Truly Mine

A Bodyguard Romance

Nichole Rose

Contents

About the Book

When the man of her dreams decides to fight fire with fire, this curvy girl might just go down in flames...

Zayne

The moment I set eyes on Emma Cooper, I knew she was meant to be mine.

Unfortunately, my shy little lamb loves the word no.

She's been rejecting me since day one.

So I'm breaking out the big guns and fighting fire with fire.

She's got too much on her shoulders.

Mine were made to support her hectic world.

By the end of the week, this curvy goddess will be mine.

Even if I have to lie my way into her life and charm her whole damn family first.

Emma

Hot, bossy, and relentless. That's Zayne Carmichael.

And the crazy man has his sights set on me.

He has no clue just how different our lives really are.

He owns his own private security company.

I spend half of every day chasing after my grandma and her sister.

Believe me, it's more complicated than it sounds. They're both eighty going on eighteen.

I know Zayne's lying when he says I'm in danger, but he insists on following me anyway.

Fine. He wants to play that game? I'll let him.

If he hasn't fled by the end of the day, it'll be a miracle.

There's just one problem.

The longer I spend with him, the less I want him to flee.

Chapter One

ZAYNE

"Crap, crap, crap."

I hide a smile behind my coffee as the curvy, raven-haired beauty picks her way across our tiled lobby in heels, wobbling like a young girl trying the shoes on for the first time. She huffs and mumbles to herself the whole time, complaining that she should have worn normal-people shoes. It's cute as hell.

I don't know why the fuck she is, but she's had my interest since she stumbled through the doors. She's stunning in a way that has my dick trying to forget that my brother is standing right beside me, prattling on about some new client.

Shit. Is she who Zion's been telling me about? I stopped listening long before she wobbled in.

But if she needs protection, I'm all over her. I mean it.

"Who is she? I want to protect her," I say, interrupting whatever the fuck Zion's saying about Adrian Kane, who used to play football for the Titans. What he has to do with anything, I don't know. He lives in a tiny town in Florida. That's not exactly close to Nashville. I'm all for expanding our private security firm, but I don't think Spring, Florida, is the location we're looking for.

Zion finally clues in on the fact that I'm not listening to a word he says and gives up talking my ear off. I don't know why he tries to tell me any of this shit anyway. I never listen.

I spent half of my life in the military. We weren't paid to ask questions. We were paid to solve problems. I don't need to know who I'm protecting. I just need to know what I'm protecting them from.

I'm not a stupid man. I'm just a simple one. Give me a job, and I'll get it done. If they want someone to blow smoke up their asses or sugar-coat the truth, I'm not the guy for the job. But if they want to make it out alive, I'm the one they call. I don't need to know a client's life story to do what needs doing.

I'm not soft and sweet. I never have been. But I know about eighty ways to kill a man. At the end of the day, that's what counts in my book.

Besides, we've got Gideon for clients who require a softer touch. He may look mean enough to spit nails, but he can make anyone feel safe.

Zion's exasperated sigh tells me maybe I should have been paying attention this time.

"I swear to Christ, Zayne. One of these fucking days, you'll actually listen to me."

"Well, that day ain't today, motherfucker." I smirk at him before taking another sip of my coffee. "Doubt it'll be the day hell freezes over, either."

He raises his hand to scratch the side of his face with his middle finger before he steps forward to meet our guest, leaving me standing there to stare at her.

I take the time to admire every inch of her. Coal-black hair tumbles in waves down her back, framing her heart-shaped face and the bluest eyes I've ever seen. Her shirt only has one sleeve, leaving her other arm and shoulder bae. Her skin looks soft as hell. And if her jeans hugged her curvy ass any tighter, it'd be a war crime.

Fuck me. She's pretty.

"Emma Cooper?"

My little lamb startles, nearly tripping over her own two feet.

My *little lamb? What the fuck?*

"Yes. Hi," she squeaks, a pretty blush painting her cheeks. "Um, are you Gideon?"

Our middle brother, Gideon, took a last-minute meeting with a country musician in need of security for some charity event.

"Zion," he says, extending his hand.

"The one Ma was supposed to swallow," I say loud enough for Zion's hearing aid to pick up.

She takes his hand, her gaze bouncing to me and then back. Shit. I think she heard me, too.

I hold her gaze, unrepentant. If she had two younger brothers, she'd probably wish her mom had swallowed them, too.

"Ignore him," Zion suggests, turning to scowl at me over his shoulder. "Everyone else does."

Ignore me? Oh, hell no.

I plop my cup down on the edge of my desk and stomp forward, not willing to be ignored this time. If she's here to hire us, my schedule is suddenly clear as glass. Gideon can have Adrian Kane or whoever Zion wants us to babysit next.

We have a rule about dating clients. It's something we all agreed we wouldn't fucking do. Ironic, considering none of us have even dated in longer than any of us should probably admit. But if this lamb needs help, I need to solve the problem quickly. The "no dating" rule doesn't apply to former clients.

"Hi, Ms. Cooper," I say, elbowing Zion out of the way. "My name is Zayne Carmichael. It's a pleasure to meet you."

"Hi," she whispers, her gaze darting from me to Zion and then back. I don't miss the way the pulse in her throat jumps as she looks at me. It damn sure doesn't do that when she looks at my little brother...though little may be a misnomer. The fucker is bigger than I am.

I hold my hand out for hers. As soon as she places hers into mine, every nerve ending in my body lights up, overloading my system with information. I process it in flickers of sensation, not sure what the fuck any of it means. But the overriding urge to lay claim to this woman like some marauder of old...that I understand. The desire screams to life, grabbing me by the balls.

The need to protect her at all costs is equally as strong, demanding I keep her safe above all else.

I bring her hand to my lips, brushing a kiss across her knuckles.

"You're safe now, lamb," I growl against her skin. "No one is going to hurt you."

She startles, her blue eyes going comically wide.

"Jesus Christ," Zion mutters. "You really don't listen, do you?"

"To you? Never. Why don't you go handle something that needs handlin', and I'll help Ms. Cooper get the intake paperwork completed?"

"Hurt me? Intake paperwork?" Emma tries to untangle her hand from mine. I hold onto it, reluctant to let her go. She's the softest thing I've ever felt, and she smells like sunshine. I didn't even know that was possible, but here we are. "Could you please let me go?"

"No."

Her pouty lips fall open in shock.

"Pretty sure you can't just touch her without permission, brother," Zion says, wry amusement lacing his tone. "It's illegal in all fifty states."

"I'm not touchin' her. I'm holding her hand."

"It's the same thing," Emma whispers.

"Nah, lamb. If I were touching you, my brother wouldn't be standin' here. I'm just keeping you safe."

Zion gapes at me like I've lost my mind.

Shit, maybe I have because I hear how batshit I sound, yet my reasoning seems perfectly rational in my mind. I don't want to let her go, and keeping her hand in mine seems like the perfect way to accomplish that.

But judging from the concerned look on Emma's face and the shit-eating grin on my brother's, I'm way off base here.

"I mean, of course, I'll let you go if you want." I reluctantly release her hand, trying to get my brain firing on all cylinders again. Jesus. I can't think through the clamor in my head.

"Thank you," she says, quickly thrusting her hand behind her back like she's afraid I'll make a play to steal it back.

"I'd say the pleasure is all mine, but it'd be a lie. Your hand is soft as hell. I much preferred when I was holdin' it."

"Jesus Christ. I cannot believe Gideon isn't here to see this shit."

"Zion? Fuck off," I growl.

He walks away, laughing to himself.

Emma looks like she's debating whether she wants to run after him.

I decide I should probably get this conversation back on solid ground before I scare her off entirely. "What is it you're needin' protection for, lamb?"

"You don't understand, Mr. Carmichael."

"Zayne."

"What?"

"My name is Zayne, baby girl."

"You don't understand, Zayne," she says, emphasizing my name in a way that makes me want to kiss the annoyed furrow from her brow. "Maybe you should listen to your brother more."

"Why? He never says anything interesting. He definitely didn't mention you being a client." That might be a lie, but I'm willing to risk my eternal soul here.

"Maybe because I'm not a client."

Thank God for small favors.

"Good. Then we can get the dating shit out of the way so I can put my ring on your finger." I grin, liking the way this is playing out. It's better than breaking the one rule my brothers and I agreed on when we started the firm. "Are you free tonight?"

"What? No." I'd be offended by the horrified look on her face if it weren't so fucking cute.

"Tomorrow night, then."

"I'm not dating you!" she cries, exasperated. "I'm here to pick up the contracts for Camila."

"Who?" I stare at her blankly.

"Camila Gomes, the publicist? She just hired your firm to provide security at events for her clients?"

Shit. Maybe I should listen to Zion more often because if this is what he was trying to tell me before Emma walked in, I heard none of it. And I don't remember Gideon mentioning it, either.

"And you work for Camila?"

"I'm her assistant," Emma says, her tone prime and fucking adorable.

Well, then it looks like Camila Gomes just hired me to personally oversee security at events. Because if Emma Cooper will be there, I damn sure will.

Chapter Two

ZAYNE

"Don't answer that!" I shout at Ma, hauling ass across the office to grab the phone from the desk before she manages to pick it up. Christ, I gotta make Zion teach me how to forward calls to my cellphone. I know he knows how. He does the shit all the time. Usually, when it's someone I don't want to deal with. Like him or Gideon.

"Don't yell at me, Zayne Matthew Carmichael!"

"Shit. Sorry, Ma."

She pats me on the shoulder and then steps aside, allowing me to snatch the phone up before one of my brothers tries to answer it from their offices.

"Carmichael Security."

The silence on the other end lets me know exactly who I'm speaking with. She never says anything when she hears my voice. I tell myself it's because she's busy thanking God she's talking to me. I have a feeling it's because she's trying to decide if she wants to hang up on me or not.

I like my version better. It sucks less than the reality where my girl has told me to go kick rocks every time we've talked since the day she walked through the doors a few weeks ago.

"Emma," I practically purr.

"How do you not have a receptionist?" she says, exasperation in her voice. "You have a fancy office and five other employees, but you're always the one who answers the phone."

I grin as her complaint rolls over me. Damn right I'm always the one who answers the phone when she calls. I've made it my life mission to be the only one she deals with around here. It's been a fun few weeks. And by *fun*, I mean if Emma doesn't cave soon, I'm going to take drastic action.

It's been three weeks since she wobbled her way into my life and turned it upside down. In those three weeks, I've asked her out at least sixty times. She's shot me down every damn time.

My dick is in danger of requiring medical intervention at this point. I've made every excuse I can to show up at Camila's office just to see her. If hiding from me was a sport, she'd medal. Half the time, she isn't even there. The other half, she vanishes like fucking Houdini.

I've never failed as epically as I'm failing when it comes to getting a date with her. And the real hell of it is that I know she's attracted to me. Those pretty blue eyes eat me up like she's trying to memorize the sight of me when we do end up in the same room together.

And I know she felt the same thing I did the first day we met. There's no way I was the only one knocked on my ass when we touched.

So why the hell won't she give me a chance?

Zion swears it's because I'm an idiot, and no one wants to date an idiot. Gideon swears it's because I'm a grumpy motherfucker, and no one wants to date a grouch. I think Ma should have swallowed them both. But maybe they're onto something because it's been three weeks, and I'm no closer to getting her to agree than I was the day she wobbled her gorgeous ass into our office.

"Good mornin' to you too, lamb."

Ma turns wide eyes on me.

I turn my back on her. She can harass me with nine thousand questions after I talk to my girl.

"Stop calling me that," Emma complains.

"I'll make you a deal," I negotiate, grinning as I clutch the receiver to my ear. "You go out with me, and I'll stop calling you that."

"I'm not going out with you, Zayne."

"Why not?"

"Because we work together."

"Zayne," Ma hisses from behind me.

I ignore her.

"Zayne!"

"Emma? Hold on a minute, baby girl."

She huffs, making me smile before I put her on hold and drop the phone back into the cradle.

"Ma, aren't you supposed to be shopping?"

"Don't tell me how to live my life, Zayne Matthew," she says, her hands on her wide hips and a scowl on her face. She comes up to my chest, but honestly, she's the scariest motherfucker I know. "Who is Emma, and why haven't I heard about her before now?"

"If you'll stop buggin' me and let me convince her that she wants to marry me, she'll be your future daughter-in-law."

Ma's eyes practically bug out of her head.

I chuckle, dropping a kiss on her head. "Go do your shopping, Ma. I'll tell you all about her at dinner."

"You better," she says, pointing a finger at me. "Or I'm telling your dad that you're being mean to me."

Shit. She probably will tell him that. Ma is a savage who takes no prisoners. She's been finessing us since we were in diapers. For someone who spends every Sunday in church, she could teach the devil a thing or two about running hell. She's sweet as pie, and as fierce as any soldier I've ever met. My brothers and I idolize her and make no secret about it.

"Go buy whatever shit you're goin' to force on us next," I say, shaking my head at her.

"If I didn't buy it for you, no one would, Zayne. You and your brothers have been single too long," she complains. "I need grandbabies. You're too old to be fun anymore."

"I'm plenty of fun."

She snorts. "You've got a stick up your butt the size of–"

I growl, cutting her off.

She grins, leaning up on her toes to kiss me on the cheek. "Whoever she is, you lit up when you realized she was on the phone," she whispers. "If she makes you look like that, I can't wait to meet her."

I drop another kiss on her head, not responding. What am I supposed to say to that? She'll love Emma if I ever convince my girl to stop telling me no. And Emma will love her too. I just need to figure out how to get Emma on the page with me because right now, we're not even in the same book.

She's a frightened little lamb, trying like hell to avoid giving me a chance. I can't figure out why and it's driving me fucking nuts.

I wait until Ma is out the front doors before I drop into the chair behind the reception desk and pick up the phone again.

"Now we're alone, and I don't have to hide how fucking hard you make me," I growl to Emma.

"You can't say that to me on the phone!"

I grin at the shy outrage in her voice. "Baby girl, if you'd agree to be mine already, I wouldn't have to say it on the phone. You keep tellin' me no."

"Zayne, I can't date you," she hisses as if she's trying not to be overheard. Is Camila in the office with her?

I briefly consider behaving and then say to hell with it. "Why the fuck not?"

"We work together."

"We'd work even better together if you were mine."

"Zayne," she groans, making me smile. "Can you please stop talking?"

"Can you please agree to go out with me?"

"No."

"Then it looks like neither of us is gettin' what we want today, lamb."

"Oh my gosh." A thump comes down the line, and then, "Ouch. That hurt."

"Did you just bang your head on your desk?"

"Maybe."

"Don't do that. You'll hurt yourself. I'll behave." *For the moment*, I add silently.

"You will?" she asks hopefully.

"Yes. What can I help you with today, Emma?"

"We still haven't received the invoice for security for Adrian Kane's book signing." As it turns out, Zion was talking about Adrian the day Emma stopped by. He's Camila's adopted brother and one of her biggest clients.

"It's already been taken care of."

"What? How? We didn't pay it, Zayne. We don't have an invoice to pay it."

"Camila may want to talk to her brother," I suggest. "He sent a check."

"Of course he did," Emma mumbles. "Camila isn't going to be happy."

"She isn't going to be happy that he paid the bill?"

"He's messing up her system again."

"Ah." I chuckle.

"Can you send me a copy of the invoice, please?"

"On one condition."

"I'm not going out with you, Zayne."

"That wasn't my condition, Emma."

"Really?" She sounds surprised. "Oh. Then what is it?"

"You answer one question for me."

Surprise turns to suspicion in the blink of an eye. "What question?"

"Would you go out with me if we didn't work together?"

Her silence is all the answer I need. Even if our company didn't handle security for Camila's clients, she'd still be telling me no. Which is all the proof I need that whatever is holding her back has nothing to do with the fact that we work together.

She's afraid of something else. I just need to figure out what the fuck it is so I can eliminate the problem.

"One of these days, you're going to stop tellin' me no, Emma," I say quietly.

"Yes. The day you finally quit asking!" she cries, exasperated. "Honestly, Zayne. I'm pretty sure this is harassment at this point."

"Is it?"

"I don't know. I'm not a lawyer." We both know it probably is, but the fact that she doesn't say it gives me hope. Deep down, she fucking loves talking to me. She's just hellbent on denying it.

"I've got another question for you, then."

Her long-suffering sigh has me grinning ear-to-ear again. She's sassy as hell, though she'd never admit it. "You ask more questions than most toddlers, Zayne."

"How else am I supposed to get to know the woman I'm going to marry?"

"You aren't. I mean, we aren't getting married." She huffs. "Stop bugging me. I have work to do."

"I haven't asked my question."

"You just asked the question."

"That was a question, lamb. It wasn't *the* question." I tip back in my chair, rocking it back and forth.

"Fine. Ask so I can do my job. Yours may be harassing people on the phone all day, but I have big girl stuff to do."

"Oh, yeah? Like what?"

"Stuff," she mumbles.

"That wasn't my question, either."

"Oh my God!"

I laugh loudly as she thumps the receiver against the desk. Talking to her is, hands down, the best fucking part of my day. I just wish like hell she'd stop running so I could do it more often.

"Ask your question, Zayne Carmichael," she says. "Before I figure out a way to strangle you through this phone."

"Do you really want me to stop askin', or are you just afraid to find out that dating me is the best decision you ever made?" I sit forward in my chair, praying to God she doesn't tell me that she wants me to quit asking. I'll respect her wishes if it's what she really wants, but I don't think it is. No, I *know* it isn't. I'm just not sure why she's fighting so fucking hard.

She hesitates for so long I'm a little worried she hung up on me. And then she gives me the only answer I need.

"Don't stop."

Chapter Three

EMMA

"Why in the world are you under your desk?" Camila asks, amusement lacing her tone as she tips sideways to peer at me like an owl.

"Shh!" I hiss, waving her away before she gets me busted. It took me ten minutes to squeeze my curvy ass under here. If Zayne finds me because she gave away my hiding spot, I'm quitting.

Okay, that's not true. I love my job and my boss. But I'll be forced to take some sort of drastic action to escape the crazy man. He won't leave me alone. Ever since Camila hired his private security firm, he's become my own personal number twenty-three. He's everywhere, all roads leading back to him.

He keeps telling me that I need to stop fighting and accept that we're going to happen.

Who says that?! Crazy people, that's who.

The first time he said it, I figured he was just being dramatic since I turned him down for a date the day we met. Except, it's been a month, and he still hasn't given up.

Every time I have to call over there for anything, he's the one who answers the phone. I swear, he does it on purpose just so he can argue with me about why I should go out with him!

When I tell him no, he gets cranky.

Have you ever tried to argue with a hot, cranky, relentless giant? Exactly! They have all the infinity stones. Which is precisely how I ended up admitting to him that I want him to keep asking me out. I didn't mean to do it!

He asked me if I wanted him to quit, and I meant to say yes. I *should* have said yes. He and I can't happen. But instead, my head and my heart went to war when he asked the question and common sense was not victorious. So I'm doing what any woman in my place would do. I'm avoiding him at all costs.

"What in the world is going on?" Camila asks, refusing to go away that easily. She plops down in my chair, lowering it as far as it'll go. "There. Now, I don't feel like I'm going to break my neck trying to see you under there." She blows a strand of hair out of her face. "Why are you hiding under your desk?"

"You didn't tell me Zayne was stopping by today," I hiss. Honestly, this is her fault. Had she warned a girl, I could have done what I've been doing for the last week and made an excuse to leave the office. Instead, he waltzed his fine butt through the door, and I skinned my knee while trying to avoid being seen.

A laugh burbles from Camila's lips. "You're hiding from Zayne?"

I poke my head out from under the desk to shoot a dirty glare up at her. "I'm not hiding."

I'm totally hiding. Zayne Carmichael is relentless and hot. I don't know what to do with either of those things! But, God, I wish I did. Every time I talk to him, he finds a way to be completely outrageous. No matter what's going on or how stressed I am, he makes me laugh. I love that so much.

"Really?" Camila makes her eyes big and looks pointedly at the small space I've managed to wedge myself into. "So whatcha doing under the desk then?"

"Looking for something I lost," I lie, patting around blindly.

"Like your mind?" She smirks at me. "Because you've definitely lost it if you think hiding under there is a better solution than talking to him, Emma."

"I can't talk to him."

"Why not?"

"Because he's hot."

"So are you."

I know I'm not ugly, but I'm not Zayne Carmichael, either. He's on Nashville's Most Eligible list, alongside every other bangable bachelor in the city. I'm a twenty-three-year-old virgin who can squeeze into a size twenty on a good day. We are not the same. I'm not even sure we're the same species, to be honest.

Zayne is intimidating. He knows exactly what he wants and goes for it. I still stutter my way through making my own appointments. He's a freaking former Marine. I barely managed to finish high school on time. His life is neat and orderly. Mine is chaos.

I spend my days chasing my eighty-year-old grandma and her twin sister. Trust me, it's harder than it sounds. They're like the geriatric version of Thelma and Louise, only I never know which of the two is responsible for talking the other into their bad ideas.

If they didn't have glaucoma, they'd watch the world burn. And if they didn't have arthritis, they'd probably dance before the flames.

As soon as the thrill of the chase wears off and Zayne realizes that our worlds are nothing alike, he'll get bored and move on to someone more his speed. That isn't me, even though a big part of me wishes it were.

The truth is...I love how relentlessly he chases me and how over-the-top he is about it. For the first time in my life, I feel like someone worthy of being pursued. He makes me feel that way.

Sometimes, I even let myself dream of what it'd be like to let him catch me. But I always wake up alone in my bed again, facing the realization that some dreams just aren't meant to be. Gran and Bets are my family, my responsibility, and it'd break my heart to fall for Zayne only for him to decide he's not ready to spend the best years of his life chasing after two crazy eighty-year-olds. And I wouldn't blame him for that. He has a business to run and his own life to live. Just because I chose this life doesn't mean I get to choose it for anyone else.

Refusing to date him is easier than getting my heart involved in something I know it won't survive. It's better for everyone to leave my heart out of the equation altogether. It can't be trusted if it's anything like my mom's, anyway.

I can't tell Camila that, though. She's one of the bravest people I know, willing to take big risks to mold her life into exactly what she wants. I don't think she'd understand why I'd rather never leave the ground than touch the sky and then have to give it up.

"We just aren't compatible," I say.

"Says who?"

"The universe." I snort, causing a piece of my hair to fly upward. "He has a company to run. I have Gran and Bets to worry about."

"You're worried he'll bail once he realizes you guys are a package deal," she says gently, immediately grasping what I don't voice.

"I just don't think my life is relationship-compatible. That's all."

"Emma."

"It's fine, Camila." I paste a smile on my face. "Honestly. I love taking care of Gran and Bets. And Zayne is *not* my type anyway. He's way too bossy for me."

He is bossy. And capable. And outspoken. And a million things I've never been. The man says exactly what he's thinking, regardless of who might hear him. He doesn't make apologies for who he is or care what anyone thinks. He's exactly who he is, no more and no less.

"Uh-huh," Camila says, not buying that for a minute. "He's not your type so much that you're hiding under the desk."

"I'm not hiding."

"Oh, yeah?" She glances up and then looks back down at me, a mischievous smirk on her face. "Then you won't mind if I'm sitting here talking to you when he comes back in, right?"

"What? Why? Is he at the door?" I squeak, trying to peer through the holes along the bottom of the desk to see. I can't, darn it all. We need more spy-worthy desks. These suck.

"Yep. He'll be walking through the doors any minute now."

"Oh, my God. Go!" I push the chair away from the desk, my heart pounding. "Before he figures out that I'm under here."

"Told you that you were hiding," she says, her laughter floating down to me as she rises from the chair.

Well, crap. I guess I walked right into that one.

"There you are."

Oh, crap on a cracker.

I spin around, holding my thermos like a deadly weapon as that familiar deep Southern growl sounds behind me. Dread shoots through me as soon as my gaze lands on Zayne stomping across the breakroom in my direction. So does an overdose of desire.

If looks could kill, I'd be dust. And if his jawline were any sharper, it'd be dangerous.

Sweet Baby Jesus. Some people really get all the luck. And by some people, I mean Zayne

Carmichael, specifically. If he's not God's favorite, he's definitely in the top three.

The man is gorgeous with his messy hair and steely gray eyes. Our breakroom looks like a freaking closet with him filling it. And it's not his size, which is impressive enough, but his *presence*. He commands attention without even saying a word.

"What are you doing in here?" I squeak. Yes, squeak like I've got something stuck in my throat. "You aren't supposed to be in here."

"Neither are you." One dark brow rises as he smirks at me. "But you've been avoiding me, so here I am."

"I have not," I lie.

"No? So you just so happened to be out of the office every time I've stopped by for the last week?"

"Camila needs lots of things." I inch along the counter, keeping space between us. "I'm her assistant. Assistants assist by running errands and getting things. It's in the job description, Zayne."

"Uh-huh. And skipping Adrian's last book signing because I was there? How do you explain that?" He keeps prowling toward me, his eyes locked on my face.

"I had things to take care of. *Personal* things," I clarify. "It had nothing to do with you." Which is actually true. Gran had her annual MRI.

"Right. And hiding under the desk when you saw me comin'? What's your excuse for that one, baby girl?"

"I wasn't hiding. I was looking for something. How was I supposed to know you were here?"

"What were you looking for?"

"Something."

"What?"

"A tampon." It's the first thing that comes to mind. I don't know why. Maybe because the universe does, in fact, hate me.

His steps falter for a minute, his lips turning up at the corners. "You were under the desk looking for a tampon?"

"Yes. I mean, no." I squeeze my eyes closed and wait for the floor to open up and swallow me, but it doesn't. In fact, my mouth just keeps going, shooting straight for trainwreck scenario. "I mean, it fell out."

Mary, Mother of God. Please make me stop talking now.

"It fell out?" His smile is so big now.

"*Of my purse*! It fell out of my purse."

"Do they fall out often?"

"Please stop talking now," I whisper, though I don't know if I'm talking to him or to myself. Either way, I really want this conversation to end immediately. I just told the hottest man I've ever met that

I was looking under my desk for a tampon that fell out.

Maybe I'm the crazy one here.

"Did you find it? Get everything taken care of down there, baby girl?"

My eyes pop open. "I'm not discussing this with you, Zayne."

"Tampons or your cycle?"

"We're not talking about either."

"Periods are normal, lamb. I'd be more concerned if you didn't have them." A little smile tugs at his lips, mischief in his gray eyes. "Although, tampons falling out may be a cause for concern too. I'll have to research and see what causes that."

He's going to *research* tampons falling out?

"Stop talking." I'm definitely talking to him this time.

The rich sound of his laugh rolls over me. "I'll stop teasing you if you agree to have dinner with me tonight."

"We've been over this. I can't date you."

"So you keep saying," he growls, quickly closing the remaining distance between us. Before I can slip past him, he's in front of me, blocking me in with one arm on the cabinet over my head. "But you had your chance to get rid of me, and you didn't take it. We both know that's because you're dying to say yes."

"No, I'm not."

"I don't know why you're fighting so hard, lamb. You know it's only a matter of time until you admit you can't breathe without me," he murmurs, leaning down over me. He's so freaking close I smell the mint of his toothpaste and the spice of his cologne. I feel the heat radiating from his body. All my senses work together. Which is to say they work against me, putting me under whatever sexual voodoo he's working on me.

"B-back up," I whisper.

"Go to dinner with me."

"I told you, I can't."

"Why not?"

"I have stuff."

"What kind of stuff?" His hand curves around my jaw, tilting my head up until our eyes meet. "What are you so afraid of?"

"N-nothing," I lie.

"Liar."

Lord, it's hard to think with him this close.

"I'm not lying, Zayne," I huff, annoyed because he's hot and close and *right*, darn it. There is a reason. There are two of them. They're eighty, and just last week, they got kicked out of a casino in Tunica for trying—and failing—to count cards. "Maybe I'd rather spend the time with my grandma than date you."

His expression softens. "You take care of your grandma?"

"Yes. And her twin sister." I lift my chin. "They live with me. So see? I'm not scared of anything. I'm just *busy*."

"Maybe that's true," he murmurs, tipping his head down as if he's telling me a secret. "But we both know the real reason you keep tellin' me no is because you felt the same thing I did that first day at my office, and it scared the shit out of you, Emma. You're trying to push me away and pull me closer at the same time, terrified that you'll make the wrong move."

"I F-felt what?"

"Like you were meant to be mine." His lips brush mine, cutting me off before I can think up a suitable denial. I feel his kiss like a gong ringing in my soul. "One day real soon, you're going to stop telling me no. When you do, I'm putting my ring on your finger and my kid in your belly."

I stand there, dumbfounded, as he drops another kiss on my lips and then winks at me.

"Have fun with your grandma tonight, lamb. I'll see you soon."

Chapter Four

ZAYNE

"What are you doing?"

"Stalking Emma."

"Why do I bother asking you questions when I know damn well you're going to tell me the truth?" Zion mutters into the phone. "I refuse to be your accomplice, motherfucker."

"Don't worry, I'm not doing anything illegal."

"Except stalking," Gideon says from beside me, peeling one eye open to look at me.

"Fucking hell. You roped Gideon into helping you?" Zion growls. "What the fuck, Zayne?"

"I'm not helping him. I'm just enjoying the shit-show."

"Uh, fuck both of you. This isn't a shitshow. I don't need help. And it's only illegal if the stalking is unwanted." I prefer to think of this as recon.

"We have got to get you a law dictionary," Gideon says around a yawn. "Stalking is stalking. It's all illegal."

"You know what I mean."

Gideon shrugs and closes his eyes again, resting his head against the windowsill. I don't think things are going well with our new client, an up-and-coming musician being stalked—*actually* stalked—by a fan. He's been in a mood all afternoon. But he's not ready to talk about whatever is on his mind, so I'm waiting him out. He'll talk when he's ready.

"Hasn't she shot you down every time you've asked her out?" Zion asks. "I'm pretty sure that puts whatever the fuck you're doing in unwanted territory."

"She takes care of her grandma and her grandma's twin sister."

"Awesome. You're going to get your ass kicked by two old women when they find out. Gideon, please record this for my posterity."

"I'm not going to get caught." I roll my eyes. "My point is that she's been turnin' me down because she's busy taking care of them."

"Or maybe she just doesn't like you."

"Plausible," Gideon agrees without even opening his eyes.

Ma really should have let me trade them for that bike I wanted from the neighbor when they were little. She wanted siblings. I wanted the bike. It was the perfect trade. Instead, Ma busted me trying to smuggle my brothers out of the house with their overnight bags. I wasn't allowed to have a bike for two years after that. And I had to keep my asshole brothers.

"Does anyone like him?" Zion asks. "Or do we just tolerate him because Ma said we have to at least pretend we like him?"

"B. The answer is B."

I ignore them, my attention focused on the colorful bungalow down the street as Emma steps out onto the front porch, wrestling with a bag of trash. It's bursting at the seams, but she hefts it as high as she can get it and hauls it down to the curb before placing it on the ground. It takes her a minute to open the garbage can and wrestle the bag inside.

By the time she gets it in there, she's panting and mumbling to herself. I smile at the sight, imagining her telling herself off for letting it get so full before she dealt with it. She may be a shy little lamb, but she's got fire in her soul.

Even dressed in fuzzy slippers and pajamas, she's fucking beautiful. I can't help but notice the little shadows under her eyes, though. She hasn't been sleeping enough. Is that because she's up late taking care of her grandmother? Does she have any help at all?

She wraps her arms around herself as if she's cold and glances around.

Shit. Does she sense me watching her?

I hunker down in my truck, hoping she doesn't notice me. Before her gaze gets to our location, though, a delivery truck rounds the corner. She turns in that direction, watching as it approaches.

The driver pulls up in front of her, obscuring my view.

"I called to tell you that you have a new client," Zion says, done talking shit about me with Gideon.

"Can't take it. Busy."

"You don't even know who it is."

"Don't care. I'm busy. You're goin' to have to handle this one."

"She's a model."

I drum my fingers on the steering wheel, impatient for the truck to move. I'm like an addict when it comes to Emma. She's been turning me down for the last month straight, but every *no* just embeds her more deeply under my skin. Every time I see her, I'm immediately looking for another reason to put myself in her general vicinity.

"Don't care," I say to Zion again. "She could be the fucking Pope, and I wouldn't care. I'm busy. You handle it." Zion doesn't take many clients. He usually runs the day-to-day operations of the business while Gideon and I handle the client work.

He was shot and left for dead five years ago in an operation gone wrong in Syria. It fucked him up for a while, left him with some permanent hearing loss. He doesn't trust his instincts like he did once upon a time, and in this line of work, your instincts are all you've got. He's a hell of a bodyguard, but we don't push him to take clients when it stresses him the fuck out.

Unfortunately, he's the last brother standing at the moment. He's going to have to take it because Gideon is dealing with the musician, Kenna. Camila just signed Gray Larsen, a member of the Nashville Predators, to her client list, which means I'll be sorting out security for him and trying to win my girl. Zion can handle the model.

"Fuck, fine," Zion growls, clearly not thrilled. "But I'm telling Ma you're stalking Emma."

"I'll tell her that you're the one who set her shed on fire." It was an accident, but I fully intend to leave that part out of the story. He was fifteen, playing with fireworks he wasn't supposed to have. One went through the window and exploded.

"That was ten years ago."

"She loved that shed," Gideon murmurs. "She could be ninety and would still be pissed."

"Fuck. You're both assholes."

"You're welcome for the model," I say before Zion hangs up on me, making Gideon chuckle.

"He's going to snap one day, and it'll be your fault."

"I didn't hear you takin' his side."

"I like stirring the pot." Gideon shrugs, his eyes still closed.

I laugh quietly. At least he's fucking honest. He does like stirring the pot. He's been doing that shit his entire life, just to see what we do. It's quality entertainment to his big ass.

My phone buzzes with an incoming message.

I grin when I read it.

Ma: Have you convinced my future daughter-in-law to like you yet?

I'm working on it, Ma.

She's been hounding me ever since I told her about Emma. She's dying to meet her, but I'm not pushing my luck. I can barely get her to stay in one place long enough for me to see her. If I throw my family at her, she may disappear to Antarctica.

Ma: Work faster. Your brothers are never going to give me grandchildren. You're my only hope.

I chuckle, tossing my phone back in the console just as the delivery truck pulls off. I sit upright, my eyes locked on Emma again. She's staring at the box in her hands, her brows furrowed. I don't know what's in it, but her expression says she's afraid it may bite her.

She spins on her heel, heading back toward her house. "Gran!" she shouts as she marches up the sidewalk. "What in the world did you order from TikTok this time? It better not be more freeze-dried candy!"

"She's cute," Gideon says.

I shoot a withering look in his direction.

"I'm just saying, I get why you're all fucked up over her," he says, shaking his head. "Jesus. I didn't say I wanted to sleep with her."

"Try it, and they'll never find your body."

A smile ghosts across his face. "So, it's like that, huh? You're serious about marrying her?"

"Yeah." Until she wobbled her way into my life, marriage and babies had never even crossed my mind. Ma wasn't kidding when she said my brothers and I have been single too long. None of us have ever made time for dating. We've always been busy with other shit, like the military and then forming the company.

Frankly, I didn't want to make time for dating. Women complicate shit without even meaning to do it, and my life was perfect exactly the way it was. But now? Well, I'm about two seconds from losing my proverbial shit just to get this woman to agree to a date.

"What are you going to do about the fact that she won't give you the time of day?"

"Don't know," I growl. "She likes me."

"You sure about that?"

I shoot him another look, which makes him chuckle.

"Want my advice?"

"Do I have a choice?"

"You invited me on this little criminal mission."

"Uh, no. You invited your damn self."

He flips me off. "Cut off her escape route," he suggests. "If you're in her face all the time and her back is against the wall, sooner or later, she'll have to stop running and face whatever the fuck is going on between the two of you."

That's...actually not terrible advice. If I'm in her personal space all the time, sooner or later, she won't be able to deny how she really feels. She'll have to deal with it. And if forcing her to spend time with me means helping her carry a little of the burden placed squarely on her shoulders? Well, that's not a bad thing either.

I just need a plan.

Luckily for me, I know a thing or two about coming up with one of those.

Chapter Five

EMMA

"Gran, I love you, but you're going to drive me to drink," I say, shaking my head at Gran, who's knitting on the sofa like I didn't receive a panicked call from Lottie, our neighbor, earlier today, informing me that they escaped and took the car again. "You and Bets have to learn to behave."

"Pah." She flaps a hand in the air. "We did that for almost eight decades. Now, we're old enough to do what the hell we want."

"You're never too old to be arrested," I remind her, chewing my bottom lip. "You can't keep driving without a license."

"Oh, hush, dear," Bets says, patting me on the hand. "We didn't even go far today. Just to Cookeville and back."

"Bets!" Gran turns a scowl on her, earning a sheepish grin from Bets.

"You *drove* to *Cookeville*?" I place my hands on my cheeks, staring at them in dismay. Cookeville is over an hour away. Way too far for the two of them to be going by themselves without a license between them. Gran got hers taken away after the stroke. I'm honestly not sure Bets ever had one to begin with. "Why in the world did you need to go to Cookeville?"

"I like the mall there," Gran says.

"Gran, we live in Nashville. There are malls everywhere!"

"They're full of tourists. I like to shop in peace and quiet, Emmaline."

I don't even want to know what she was shopping for today. There's no telling with her. My grandparents never had much. Grandpa worked every day for every penny they had. But when he died, he left Gran a millionaire. I don't think she even knew about the massive life insurance policy he'd taken out on himself until the day we found the paperwork.

What he couldn't give her in life, he's more than making up for in death. Gran and Bets shop like they're professionals and love every minute of it. It's terrifying, honestly.

"Oh! That reminds me." Gran sets her knitting aside and hauls herself off the sofa before hobbling toward the kitchen, only to return a few moments later with a bag under her arm. "I picked this up for you today."

I carefully reach into the bag, retrieving the book tucked inside. "Good Girls Get Punished," I read the title aloud, my eyes widening at the mostly naked man on the cover. "Good lord. I think the towel in front of his package may be the only thing keeping it from saluting the whole world."

"They really ought to make book covers like they do those moving images on your computer," Bets says, peering over my shoulder. "I'd like to see what he can do when he drops that towel."

"Bets!" I cry, shoving the book back into the bag as my cheeks burn.

Gran cackles, slapping her knee.

"Well, don't blame me!" Bets huffs. "If he's going to put it out there, I have a right to wonder, don't I?"

"You have got to stop reading dirty romance," I tell her before turning narrowed eyes on Gran. "And you have to stop driving. If you want to go shopping while I'm at work, all you have to do is let Lottie know. She'll take you."

Lottie helps keep an eye on Gran and Bets while I'm working. At least she tries to keep an eye on them for me. They tend to escape before she real-izes they're gone more often than not. It's not her fault. They're crafty for old ladies.

"Lottie drives like she's got one foot in the grave," Gran says.

"And she listens to that God-awful screaming racket," Bets agrees, her lips pursed just like Grans. Aside from the fact that Bets wears her hair long while Gran prefers to keep hers permed, there's no telling them apart. They're identical, right down to the little birthmarks on their left earlobes.

"It's rap," Gran says.

"It is not rap. That sweet boy with the bad tattoos is rap. What's his name, dear?" she asks me. "Toast Throne?"

"Toast Throne? Do you mean Post Malone, Bets?"

"Yes! That's the one." She beams at me. "Such a sweet boy."

How does she even know enough about Post Malone to have an opinion of his character? *I* don't even know enough about him to have an opinion. Actually, I don't want to know how she knows about him. Some questions are better left unanswered.

"Maybe we should find you a nice musician," Gran muses. "You can't carry a tune in a bucket. Having someone around here who can sing would be nice."

"I don't want a musician."

"Doctor?" Bets suggests.

"At least they'd be useful if we keel over," Gray murmurs, picking up her knitting again.

"No."

"Lawyer?"

"That'll come in handy next time you get a ticket, Lou."

"No."

"Hon, are you sure you even like men?" Gran asks me, straight-faced. "It's all right if you don't, you know."

"Gran, I'm straight."

"Are you sure? You've never even been on a date with a man, let alone gotten busy with one."

"Are you suggesting she should sleep with a man to find out if she likes it?" Bets asks.

"I'm just making an observation, but if she wants to take one for a test drive before committing to a purchase, well, I suppose that's her prerogative, isn't it?"

"Yes, I'm sure!" I cry, hiding my face in my hands. Maybe I should take up drinking. I don't even like the taste of alcohol, but surely, it's no worse than listening to Gran and Bes talk about my lack of a sex life. "I met someone."

Crap. I didn't mean to say that.

"Oh, dear," Gran whispers. "You've gone and fallen in love, haven't you?"

"What?" I pull my hands away from my face. "No."

"Oh, she has!" Bets cackles. "That's why she's been so cranky lately, Lou!"

"Who is he?" Gran asks.

"Does he look like the guy on that book cover?"

"Oh, my God." There's no way I'm telling either of these crazy women about Zayne. Knowing my luck, they'll be on his doorstep within the hour, demanding to know his intentions. Or, worse, demanding to know the condition of his package. Gran wasn't lying when she said they were old enough to do what they wanted. It's her motto in life now. And I'm pretty sure it's always been Bets' motto. "Can we *please* talk about something else? This doesn't even matter."

"Why not?"

"Because it's never going to happen!"

Gran and Bets share a look before Gran reaches for my hand. "Come sit down with me, dear."

I reluctantly let her lead me to the couch, flopping down gracelessly...only to grimace when a knitting needle jabs me in the butt cheek. I retrieve it, setting it aside.

"Why don't you want to talk about your young man, Emmaline?"

"Because he's not mine, Gran," I sigh. "He's just a guy at work."

"A client?"

"No. He runs a private security company that Camila contracts."

Gran nods knowingly. "And he has a stick up his butt and doesn't know you exist? Your grandpa was the same way when we first met."

I snort, finding that hard to believe. Grandpa worshipped the ground Gran walked on, and everyone knew it. The man didn't have a poetic bone in his body, but he wrote her the sweetest love letters.

"Zayne knows I exist," I mutter. "The man won't leave me alone."

Gran and Bets share another look. I swear, they've honed their twin powers over the last eighty years. They say more to each other with a look than most people say in an hour of conversation. It's terrifying, really.

I'm not sure what they're saying now, but Gran wraps an arm around my shoulders, running her fingers through my hair. "Then maybe you should stop fighting to resist him and find out why he's so keen to chase, dear girl. Before you miss out on something you can't get back."

"She's right." Bets bobs her head in an emphatic nod. "You don't want to end up old and alone like me, do you?"

"You aren't alone, Bets. You have us."

She smiles at me, but it doesn't reach her eyes like usual. "And I wouldn't change a minute of it. But there are some mistakes you can't take back, sweet girl. I know because I made the same one you're making now. I fought it until I chased my man clean out of town. He went off to war, never knowing how I felt about him."

"Bets." My expression falls. I didn't know that. I always thought she never got married because she never wanted to be tied down. She's always been independent, seemingly content on her own. "Did he...did he die overseas?"

"What? Good heavens, girl, no. The man came home and decided to go to work robbing banks."

"Bets, I don't think this story is having the intended impact," I say wryly. It sounds more like she might have dodged a bullet if you ask me.

"War changes people, Emmaline. The man who came back from that war wasn't the one I fell in love with. Who knows how life would have turned out if I'd just bent a little?" she asks. "Maybe his life would have been different."

"Maybe you'd have been a bank robber too."

"It worked for Bonnie and Clyde, didn't it?"

"What? No! No, it did not work for Bonnie and Clyde," I say, laughing in disbelief. "Their story ended with everyone dying."

"Perhaps, but it ended with them together." Bets' eyes twinkle. "That has to count for something."

I never pegged my aunt as a hopeless romantic, but I think she may be the biggest romantic I know. I'm not entirely convinced she's right about dying together in infamy being the way to go, but maybe she and Gran have a point.

I've been fighting so hard to protect my heart from Zayne...but what if doing it means leaving his open to be broken? Is that really the weight I want to carry for the rest of my life?

"We need to talk."

"We're talking now, Zayne," I say, holding the phone between my shoulder and ear while I work on proofing the press release Camila dropped on my desk a few minutes ago.

"In person."

"We just talked in person the day before yesterday," I remind him. "You cornered me in the breakroom and kissed me." He may have forgotten, but I certainly haven't. Ever since my talk with Gran and Bets, I've thought about nothing but him and those two kisses. They've become the star of very vivid, very frustrating dreams, as a matter of fact.

"That wasn't a kiss. That was a goodbye. When I kiss you, you'll know it."

"Your lips touched mine." I glance around furtively to make sure Camila isn't close enough to overhear. I haven't told her about the kisses yet. "That's the definition of a kiss."

"Yeah? Want to test that theory?"

The little bell over the front door chimes, pulling my attention. When I glance up, one very hot giant is standing there, looking incredibly smug. And way too hot in a three-piece suit. He makes the body-guard uniform look way too freaking good.

"Hello, lamb," he drawls.

How in the world did he call from his office number if he's on a cellphone? This is not how phones are supposed to work!

"You're supposed to be at your office," I complain into the phone.

"Forwarded the number." He smirks, leaning against the door frame. "You think I've been an-swerin' the phone every time you call by accident?"

"No. I thought I was just unlucky," I grumble, earn-ing an even bigger smile from him. "Why did you call me if you were already here?" And why am I still talking to him on the phone when he's standing in front of me? Jeez.

I drop the phone into the cradle a little harder than necessary.

He chuckles before pulling his away from his ear to tuck it into his breast pocket. "I called to distract you so you'd keep your pretty little ass at your desk this time until I made it in the building. Wouldn't want you losing another tampon under that desk, baby girl."

"Oh, my God. Please leave my office."

"No, can do." He sobers, the smile sliding from his face. "We have to talk."

"We've been doing that for five minutes now."

"This is serious."

"So is this." I swipe the press release off my desk and wave it in the air. "Have you ever tried to proofread for Camila? She throws commas around like they're glitter. And we need to get this out immediately."

Our new client, Gray Larsen, has had some trouble with the press recently after a disastrous Win-a-Date contest. His date got sloshed, and tried to proposition him. She then puked on his shoes while he was trying to get her into a cab to get her home, which a few lucky photographers caught on camera. It's been all over the gossip pages lately.

Everyone is poking fun at him. Which would be fine and dandy, except a few have started to question if he did something to get her to that state. He didn't, but it doesn't take much for an athlete to end up with a bad reputation, even if it's undeserved.

Gray doesn't deserve it. He's a great guy. He's also a fantastic hockey player. He just happens to be a certified disaster off the ice. He needs all the help he can get turning the press in his favor. Camila sent him camping with the Boy Scouts the other day to help rehab his tarnished image. It didn't go well. He ended up with poison ivy in unmentionable places.

He's very dramatic!

"Fine. Finish proofreading, and then we'll talk."

I narrow my eyes on Zayne. "I can't work if you're watching me."

"Why not?"

"It's weird."

"It's weird to read while I sit here quietly and enjoy the view?" He lowers himself into the chair across from my desk, keeping both eyes focused on me the entire time. There's no mistaking the heat in his gaze, as if he fully intends for me to know just how much he enjoys the view.

It's mind-boggling to me that a man who looks like him looks at me the way he does. He's completely gorgeous, but he stares at me as if I'm the most beautiful thing he's ever seen. I don't think anyone has ever looked at me quite like he does.

I give up trying to get him to go away. It's pretty evident he's going to do the exact opposite of anything I say. When I said he was relentless, I wasn't kidding.

"How long were you a Marine?"

"Ten years. Why?"

"Just trying to figure out if they made you this annoyingly stubborn or if it's a requirement to join up," I say sweetly, earning a belly laugh from him.

"Baby, I was born this way. Ask my ma."

"You call her Ma?" I smile despite myself. Of course, he calls her Ma instead of Mom. He's about as Southern as they come. Why is that so attractive to me?

"She'd kick my ass if I called her anything else."

My smile turns into a full-blown grin. "You're scared of your mom."

"Hell yeah, I'm afraid of Ma. She's five-foot-nothing and meaner than a junkyard dog."

"No, she is not."

He cracks a smile. "Nah, she's sweet as pie. But she'd fuck me up in a heartbeat. She raised three boys. She doesn't know the definition of backing down."

"She sounds awesome."

"She thinks you sound awesome."

I fumble my pen, leaving a line of red ink across Camila's release. "You told your mom about me?"

"Mmhmm."

Oh, my word. This man really is going to be the death of me.

"Zayne! You can't go telling your mom about me like we're dating. We aren't dating."

"Trust me, I'm aware," he growls, pouting like a little boy who didn't get his way. "Ma is ready to kick my ass because you've shot me down seventy-three times in a row."

"Seventy-three... Have you been *counting*?"

He jerks his chin in a nod. "Gideon thinks you'll make it a square one hundred. Zion has his money on one fifty."

"Wait. You guys are betting on how many times I'll turn you down?"

"Me? Fuck no. But they think it's hilarious that you're hellbent on givin' me a complex. I don't suppose you want to do me a favor and say yes so they shut the fuck up already?"

"I..." I shake my head, at a loss for words. He told his mom about me, and she thinks it's his fault I won't date him. His brothers are betting on how many times I'll turn him down. *He talks to his family about me.* What am I supposed to say to that?

"Finish your proofreadin', lamb."

I leap at the chance to exit the conversation, my mind reeling. For weeks now, I've been trying to convince myself that I'm just a passing curiosity for him and that he'll get bored and move on soon. I've been clinging to that as if it'll spare my heart. But he just stole a big chunk of it anyway.

I haven't given a single inch, and he's already talking about me to the people who matter to him. If I were just a notch on his bedpost, I don't think he'd be doing that. Maybe it's not like that in most places, but in the South, getting families involved is serious.

Yesterday, when Bets raised the possibility that I could break his heart, I almost talked myself out of believing it. But the proof is right here, staring me in the face.

And that's somehow even more terrifying than the possibility of him breaking my heart. I know nothing about love, relationships, or dating. I've avoided all possibilities of them, throwing myself into caring for Gran and Bets so I didn't have time to think about it. So long as they were my priority, I could convince myself that there was no room in my life for anyone else. I didn't have to face reality.

And the reality is this: everything I know about love ends in grief. My dad loved my mom fiercely, right up until she destroyed him and then got them both killed. Gran loved Grandpa madly, right up until he died, leaving her spinning like a top. I run because it's easier than facing the possibility that I might end up facing the same thing. Or, worse, that I might be just as destructive and selfish as my mom.

The *last* thing I want to do is hurt this man. But what if that fatal flaw was encoded in my DNA, passed down from her? It's a terrifying possibility, the one that keeps me up at night.

I have to read through the press release three times before I manage to successfully proof it. My mind keeps bouncing back to the man sitting across from me, patiently waiting for me to finish. But on the third pass, I've given up trying to figure out what the right thing to do is here, and I'm mostly confident I finally got all of Camila's wayward commas. I reluctantly set it beside a paperweight shaped like a hair bow, blowing out a breath.

"What do you want to talk about?"

"You're in danger."

I blink at him. "Excuse me?"

"You're in danger," he says again.

"I'm in danger? What are you talking about?" I narrow my eyes on him. "Did you hit your head or something?"

"No."

"Are you on drugs?"

"Fuck no," he snorts.

"Then you're just plain crazy. I'm not in danger, Zayne."

"You are. Someone hired me to provide security services to you because they have reason to believe you're in danger."

"What? Who hired you?"

"I'm not at liberty to discuss that information."

I gape at him, incredulous. "You're kidding me right now. Did Camila put you up to this?"

"No. I haven't spoken with Camila about it yet. Her office is my next stop."

"Tell me who hired you." I narrow my eyes on him. "Zayne Carmichael, did you hire yourself to follow me around?"

"No."

I scrutinize his expression, trying to figure out if he's lying to me or not. His level expression doesn't change, though. Either he's telling the truth, or he's impressively good at lying with a straight face.

The only people I know who would even think of hiring him to follow me around are him and Camila. Him because he's crazy and her because she's dying to know what's going on between us.

I'm not sure who that leaves.

My eyes widen. "Holy crap. Did my grandma or aunt talk you into this?"

"No."

"Did you talk them into it? Because I swear to God, I will strangle you if you've got them thinking I'm in danger!"

It took two months to convince Gran to give up the expired bear spray she's been carrying in her purse for the last decade. God only knows what she'll do if she thinks I'm in danger. And Bets wasn't exactly on the side of rationality yesterday when it came to Bonnie and Clyde. Who knows what she's capable of doing?

"I've never even spoken to your grandmother or aunt, baby girl," he says quietly.

So he's making it up then.

Why?

I don't understand why this man is willing to go to such lengths to spend time with me. He doesn't even know me. And yet...and yet he's telling his family about me. And yet he still shows up here with excuses as to why he needs to see Camila even though he rarely even makes it to her office. And yet, he hasn't given up.

"What does having a bodyguard entail, exactly?" I ask, not entirely sure what I'm thinking. Not entirely sure I haven't lost my mind, too. But I'm tired of trying to resist this man when every cell in my body screams for something different. So maybe it's time to switch tactics.

If he wants to invade my life...maybe it's time I let him. Once he sees exactly what he's up against, he'll leave me alone, or he won't. One way or another, I'll know, right?

God, why is that such a terrifying prospect to me?

"A bodyguard makes sure you have everything you need to ensure your safety. He deals with any threats and handles anything or anyone that needs handling. Most importantly," he says, his eyes roaming down my chest, "a bodyguard guards your body."

Oh, really?

"Then I just have one question." I wait until he meets my gaze again to ask it, making sure he knows that I know he's full of it, and I'm willing to fight just as dirty as he is. "Which of your brothers is it going to be?"

The dark growl that erupts from his throat is as menacing as it is hot. "If either of my brothers even thinks about guarding your body, Ma won't ever find theirs, lamb."

Well, okay then.

He rises from his chair, circling around the desk to me. I spin in my chair, trying to keep two eyes on him just in case he tries to kiss me again. But this time, he simply leans down over me, putting his mouth next to my ear.

"Keep fucking with me about other men, and I'll tie you to the bed and turn your curvy ass red," he growls. "Right before I wipe the memory of every name you could even think to suggest from every inch of your mind. You're mine, and *I don't share.*"

Did he just threaten to tie me up and spank me? Better question. Did I like it?!

Crap. I did. I really, *really* did.

His lips brush my cheek before he snatches the press release off my desk. "I'll take this to Camila while you finish up for the day."

Chapter Six

ZAYNE

"Maybe you can start tomorrow," Emma says for the fifth time since we left the office half an hour ago. It took some convincing—a lot of convincing—but she finally agreed to let me drive her home. I didn't really leave her much of a choice when I stole her car keys out of her purse and refused to give them back. As of now, I'm on duty. Guarding her body. Best assignment ever. "There's no reason to rush into this."

"There's every reason," I disagree. "You need a bodyguard."

If hell is real, I'm going there for lying to her. I've accepted this. But Gideon suggested I cut off her escape route and force her to deal with me. What better way than by appointing myself as her bodyguard? Actually, I didn't appoint me. That wasn't technically a lie.

Gideon hired me to protect her. She doesn't need to know that he used my money—quite happily, I might add.

And she is in danger. She's in danger of breaking my fucking heart. She's in danger of running herself ragged. She's in danger of getting herself fucked through the mattress if she doesn't stop being so goddamn cute. But she didn't ask what kind of danger she was in, so I didn't technically lie about any of that either.

It's ice thin enough to count as frost. But desperate times call for desperate measures. She's been running for long enough. It's time for her to realize that whatever the fuck she's so afraid of isn't going to happen.

"You can start tomorrow."

I pull up alongside the curb outside her house and kill the engine. "Okay, so, we need to get a few things straight, lamb."

"Good idea," she says, her voice colored with relief. "We should probably come up with a reason why I need a bodyguard that doesn't involve me being in danger. I don't think either of them owns a gun, but I'm also not entirely convinced they don't know where to go buy one, either."

I lift a brow. That was not one of the things I meant we needed to get straight, but it's good to know her grandma and aunt are bad-asses who may or may not shoot me if I fuck this up.

"How old did you say they are?"

"Eighty." Her shoulders slump. "Um, I should warn you before you go in that they're both feral, and I have no control over anything that comes out of their mouths. Believe me, I've tried. But when you're that old, I guess you get to say whatever you want. At least, that's what Gran always tells me." She shrugs, looking slightly sick. "So I'm sorry in advance if they say anything inappropriate. And ignore any questions about your...um..." Her gaze drops to my lap, heat climbing into her cheeks. "Well, just ignore any questions, okay?"

Jesus Christ. The more she talks, the more I can't wait to meet these two.

"I'll take that under consideration," I say to ease her mind, though I have no intention of following through. I'll answer any questions they have. Unless she's serious about them asking about my dick. I'm not fucking whipping it out for two old ladies to inspect or some shit.

Fucking hell. Surely, she isn't suggesting that's a possibility...right?

Either her life is far more interesting than mine, or she needs a whole helluva lot more help around here than I realized.

"My rules are simple, lamb," I murmur. "What I say goes. No trying to ditch me. No puttin' yourself in danger. We're doing things my way now."

"I already don't like your rules," she mumbles just loud enough for me to hear.

"Then you'll really hate the last one."

"There's more?" She sounds horrified, and I've never wanted to eat someone more.

"Mmhmm. You need to tell your grandma that we're dating. It'll make her hate me far less when I'm sleeping on your couch tonight." It'll also give me an excuse to touch Emma whenever the fuck I want. Dick move? Probably. Am I sorry? Absolutely not.

"S-sleeping on my couch?" Emma squeaks. "You didn't say anything about sleeping on my couch, Zayne! I didn't agree to this!"

"I can't guard your body from across town, little lamb." I cup her cheek, gently closing her mouth with my thumb. I'd much prefer to guard it while she's wrapped around me in her bed. But I have a feeling I may not survive the next five minutes if I suggest that, so I don't go there. Yet.

But is it really my fault if a motherfucker gets lost looking for the bathroom in the middle of the night? No, no, it's not.

"Come on. Let's go meet Gran and Bets." I slide out of the truck before she decides to call this whole thing off. I think she knows I'm full of shit.

She's played along this far because her resolve is weakening, but if I push too far, I may just push her curvy ass right out of the door.

"Zayne!" she hisses at me.

I slam the door, pretending not to hear her.

"I'm going to murder you in your sleep!" she shouts, making me laugh as I circle the truck to help her out.

"Watch your step, baby girl," I murmur. "Matter of fact..." I slide my hands around her waist, lifting her from the truck. She grabs onto my shoulders as if she thinks I'm going to drop her. But I've carried bloody, battered Marines out of the worst shitholes on this planet without faltering. There's not a chance in hell I'll drop the most important thing I've ever held in my arms.

"Put me down," she says breathlessly, her blue eyes locked on my face.

"Mm. Holding you is doing a number on my cock, but damn if I don't love every fuckin' second of it."

"You can't talk to me like that."

"Yeah? Says who?"

"Me."

"In that case..." I nudge the truck door closed and press her up against it. "Maybe I forgot to mention that other rule."

"Another rule? What rule?"

"The one where I'll say whatever filthy thing I want to say when we're alone," I growl, running my lips down the side of her throat. "My mouth, my choice, baby girl. And I choose to use it to tell you how fucking crazy you make me."

"Zayne," she moans, pliant in my arms. "We're outside."

"Believe me, I'm aware." I nuzzle her neck, growling. "Fuck, you smell edible. Do you bathe in sugar?"

"What? No. Who does that?"

"You taste like it." I nip her throat with my teeth, trying not to dry hump the hell out of her in front of the entire neighborhood. And then I reluctantly pull back. "Let's get you inside before you make me do something you'll regret."

"I'm not responsible for your actions, Zayne Carmichael."

"You are when you're squirming on my cock like you can't wait to feel me inside you, lamb."

She groans loudly, burying her face in my throat as I carry her toward the house, but she doesn't demand I put her down again. I like this cuddly side of her. She's sweet as hell in my arms.

Right up until we reach the end of the sidewalk and she remembers where we are, anyway. As soon as she does, she manages to slip out of my arms, damn near landing on her ass before she catches herself.

"Crap. I should have thought that through better," she huffs, blowing a strand of hair out of her face to peer up at me. "Stop working your sexual voodoo on me. I need to focus."

"On what?"

She opens her mouth like she's going to respond and then snaps it closed with a shake of her head. "Never mind, I'll just show you." A second later, she scurries up the steps and then flings open the door. "Gran, Bets, are you decent?"

"We haven't been decent since the sixties, girl!" an old lady calls back.

Another one cackles.

"That's what I need to focus on," she mutters.

I fight a smile, following her into the house...praying to God her grandmother and aunt are actually dressed, and I'm not about to see something I'll never recover from.

To my relief, they're fully clothed. Though, one of the old ladies is in a hot pink muumuu, and the other is wearing almost exactly what Richard Simmons wore in most of his videos. I'm not sure which twin is which, but they look identical to me. The house is...interesting. I suppose that's a word for it. The furniture is an eclectic mix of antiques in all shapes and sizes. Bright paintings mix with more subdued pieces and family photos all over the walls. The only things that match are the colorful area rugs.

"Well, I'll be," the twin in the '80s workout gear breathes, her eyes wide as she looks me over. "You could be on one of those book covers, couldn't you?"

"Bets," Emma groans. "Please behave."

"I ain't said nothing he can't see with his own two eyes, girl," Bets says, waving Emma off. "I'm sure the man owns a mirror."

Emma groans, looking at me with big eyes. "Zayne, this is my Aunt Betty Cooper, Bets for short."

"It's nice to meet you, ma'am. I've heard a lot about you."

"Don't believe a word of it either," Bets says. "And don't start with that ma'am shit. You call me Bets or Aunt Bets. I'm too old to be reminded how old I am."

"Yes, ma...I mean Bets," I say, grinning. She's feisty. I'm guessing that's exactly where Emma gets it from. My girl has fire in her soul and the devil in her eyes. I glance from Bets to Emma's grandmother. "You must be Ms. Cooper."

"Ms. Cooper, is it? Ain't had anyone call me that in sixty years."

"Sixty years, huh? Then my eyes must be deceivin' me because you can't possibly be a day older than that."

Her blue eyes light up as she cackles like I just made her day. "Oh, I like him," she says to Emma. "You should definitely keep doing what you were doing outside if it means he keeps saying such nice things to two old ladies, dear."

"What we were doing...?" Emma claps her hands on her red cheeks. "Were you spying on us through the window, Gran?"

"Of course we were, dear."

I scratch my face to hide a smile. I like these two already. They're hell on wheels and clearly not sorry about it.

"Gran! You can't just spy on me. It's rude."

"Pah." The old lady waves her hand in the air like she's swatting at a bug. "Don't start that baloney with me, Emmaline. If you didn't want us watching, you shouldn't have been doing it on the street."

Emma shoots a death glare in my direction, telling me without words that this is all my fault. I'm willing to take the blame. Her grandma doesn't sound upset about the fact that I was all over her granddaughter. In fact, she sounds...amused.

"So, you're the one she's been so worked up over, huh?" Gran says to me.

"I have not been worked up over him!" Emma objects.

I grin from ear to ear as her face burns bright red. Seems my little lamb has been telling tales about me to her grandma and aunt. Fuck. Why does that make me feel like a goddamn king?

"Whatever you say, dear." Gran pats her on the arm before turning back to me. "Are you staying for dinner? Or did she recruit you to babysit us like she did the neighbor? We might be convinced to behave for you, but it's not likely."

"I imagine the two of you behave just fine without a babysitter."

Emma snorts, letting me know that's absolutely not the case. Unless I miss my guess, they probably run circles around her. It's obvious that she adores them. It's equally as obvious that old age hasn't slowed them down any at all. She's got her hands full between the two of them and her job.

Shit. No wonder she's busy all the time. Poor lamb is probably exhausted.

"He's going to be here for a while, Gran," Emma says.

"Is he? Why?"

Emma looks at me, clearly at a loss how to explain my presence. I consider forcing the dating story, but decide to cut Emma a little slack. At least for the moment.

"I'm Emma's bodyguard."

"Her bodyguard?" Gran's brows climb toward her hairline. "Is that what you kids are calling it nowadays?"

"Gran!"

"Well, I'm just asking."

I fight a smile.

"I told you that he owns a private security firm with his brothers."

"Brothers? Do they look like him?"

"No. My brothers are hideous trolls," I lie without shame. Just in case they decide they don't like me and want to get one of them over here instead. "Mean, too."

Bets grins like she knows exactly what I'm doing, but she doesn't call me on my bullshit. She's an old lady after my heart.

"So you need a bodyguard now? I swear, you kids start hanging around someone famous, and suddenly, the whole world knows who you are. Doesn't anyone have any privacy anymore?" Gran complains. "Bets, remember that summer you spent on Teddy Wilkins's tour bus? No one bothered you."

"I'm not hanging around the Predators, Gran. Gray is our newest client." She turns wide eyes on Bets. "And why didn't I know you spent a summer touring with Teddy Wilkins?"

I don't know much about music, but everyone in Nashville knows Teddy Wilkins. The man was a legend and more rock n' roll than anyone in country music during his heyday. If Bets was on tour with the man, I'm guessing she's seen some things.

"You aren't old enough to hear that particular story, dear." Bets pats her hair, refusing to meet her niece's gaze.

"I'm twenty-three!"

"Yes, that's not nearly old enough," Gran says. "Ask her again in ten years."

Jesus. Emma wasn't kidding when she said they're feral. Watching them is like watching a ping pong match, only no one knows the rules, the score, or where the damn ball went.

"So what does being her bodyguard entail, sweet boy?" Gran asks me, changing the subject before Emma can object to being classified as too young to hear her aunt's exploits. Though, frankly, I think *I* may be too young to hear them.

"Routine shi...stuff," I amend quickly, trying to mind my manners. Ma would kick my ass for cursing in front of these two. "I'll be moving in while I update security around here and keep an eye on things."

"Moving in?" Emma wheels around to face me, her eyes wide. "You are not moving in."

"Yeah, I am, baby girl."

"I did not agree to this."

"My rules, my way, remember?" I run my thumb down the side of her cheek. "You agreed when you agreed to that."

"I didn't agree to that! You distracted me until I forgot to argue."

"Oh, I like him," Bets whispers to Gran, linking her arm through her sister's. "He's a smart one."

"Stop siding with the enemy, Bets. You're supposed to be on my team."

"Emmaline, dear girl, if being on your team means this gorgeous man isn't moving in, no one wants to be on your team," Bets says frankly, patting her niece on the head. "But you two keep arguing about it. Lou and I will get dinner started."

Chapter Seven

ZAYNE

"I am so mad at you," Emma hisses as soon as Gran and Bets exit the room. "You told them you're moving in."

"I am moving in."

"I didn't agree to this."

"You did. You just don't remember doing it," I lie, reaching for her. She tries to evade me by dodging to the left, but I manage to get my hands on her anyway.

She huffs as I haul her into my arms, effectively trapping her up against my body.

"You're sexy as hell when you're pissed, lamb."

"Stop flirting with me, Zayne. I'm trying to be annoyed with you."

"Yeah? How's that working out for you?" I ask, undoing the twist holding her hair up on her head. The thick mass goes tumbling down her back. I immediately plunge my hands into it, my dick pulsing. Fucking hell, even her hair is soft.

"It was easier when I was over there," she mutters, making me chuckle.

"I can move us over there if you think it'll help."

She turns that adorable scowl up at me. And that's about all I can take. I've been trying to get my hands on this woman for a fucking month, driving myself crazy thinking about what I'd do once I had her in my arms. Now she's here, and I'm not wasting another damn second.

I swoop, claiming her mouth before she even has a chance to resist me. To my surprise, she doesn't even try. She whimpers, the sound shooting straight to my cock. Her hands get tangled in my hair as she tries to pull me closer.

I lick into her mouth, attacking it like I would her pussy. Fucking hell. She tastes like magic. Her taste hits my system, annihilating any chance I had of surviving this if she kicks my ass to the curb. Did I even stand a chance of surviving it anyway?

No.

I think I knew on day one that she was it for me. It's why I've been fighting so hard to get her on the same page. I'm a simple man with simple needs.

And I knew five minutes after meeting her that I needed her in my life.

That sense of certainty has only grown in the last month.

She's vital to me now, ranking above everything else on Maslow's Hierarchy of Needs. If we require a purpose, she's mine. If life needs meaning, it's her.

"Jesus, lamb," I rasp, breaking from her lips only to come back to them again and again. I can't stop kissing her now that I've started. She certainly isn't telling me no. It's a far cry from the last month. Her surrender is the sweetest victory I've ever tasted.

"You have to stop kissing me," she mumbles, biting my bottom lip. "You're going to get us caught again."

I solve that problem lickety-split. I walk her backward toward the narrow hallway on the opposite side of the living room. Somehow, I manage to avoid the antique coffee table and the pile of yarn spilling from a basket beside the sofa.

Gran and Bets chatter away in the kitchen, happily banging pots and pans as they bicker over who makes the best garlic bread. Confident they'll be occupied for at least the next few minutes, I drag Emma into the first room I come across, slamming the door behind us.

I catch a brief flash of a gray and yellow shower curtain and matching rug before the small bathroom is plunged into complete darkness.

"Now, we won't get caught," I growl, fumbling for the lock on the door just to cover all my bases.

"Zayne," Emma whispers, a nervous tremble in her voice. I hear the excitement in it, too. She wants this. She's just afraid to reach for it.

"Shh, lamb." I press her back against the door, nuzzling her neck. "I've got you."

"I...I..."

"Do you want me to stop?"

"No."

I exhale a breath, proud as hell of her. She's shy and sweet and nervous as hell. But she's eager to explore what's between us, aching for me to show her how good it can be. I think she's just afraid to place her heart into my hands when she'd be giving me the power to crush it.

She should know by now, though, that these hands were made to protect every piece of her. They were made for worshipping every part of her. I don't give a fuck how hectic her life is or how wild her aunt and grandma are, or how far she runs; I'm not going anywhere.

"Then lean back and let me show you what you've been itchin' for since I kissed you in the break-room." I trail kisses down the tantalizing hint of cleavage her shirt reveals. The way she dresses drives me crazy. She doesn't try to hide her curvy body. She isn't ashamed of it. She dresses to accentuate the extra God gave her. And fuck me, every time I see her, I want to hit my knees and say a prayer for women designed like her.

"I thought you said those weren't kisses."

"I lied," I growl, tugging the top of her shirt down to kiss along the tops of her breasts. Jesus. I can't wait to get my mouth on them. I skim one hand down her side, loving the way she shivers and moans at my touch. Loving how fucking soft she is.

"At least you ad-admit it," she gasps.

"Admit what? That I'm willing to do whatever it takes to make you mine?" I press my body close to hers, letting her feel how fucking hard she makes me. "That I'll lie, cheat, and steal my way into your heart if that's what it takes to get in there?" I nip her bottom lip, slipping my hand down her skirt. "That I've spent the last few days jerking myself raw thinking about those kisses?" My lips slide down the side of her throat, seeking out the pulse pounding there. "I admit to all of it, lamb. You drive me fuck-ing crazy."

"You make me crazy...Oh my God!" She practical-ly faceplants in my shoulder when I cup her pussy through her panties, not being gentle about it.

"This is mine, baby girl," I growl. And then I press my free hand over her heart. "And this is mine too. I intend on claiming both."

"Zayne," she whispers, her voice strangled.

"You want to come?"

"Y-yes. No. I don't know!"

Ah, fuck.

"You're a virgin, aren't you, lamb?"

"Yes," she whispers.

If this isn't proof she was made for me, nothing is. She's been waiting to give it to me, same as I've been waiting for her.

I flick her panties to the side, on a motherfucking mission now. "You really shouldn't have told me that if you wanted to keep me out of here," I murmur against her skin, running my thumb up her bare slit. "You'll be lucky if you make it through the night without me slippin' into your bed to claim it."

"Please. Oh, please." Her little claws dig into my shoulders, delivering a delicious bite of pain as I touch her for the first time. I want to see her, want to memorize every expression that crosses her face, but I leave the lights off, knowing just how powerful one sense can become when you lose another. I want her to feel every second of this.

I toy with her, touching every part of her hot little cunt. She's dripping for me, sticky sweet, and practically begging for me to take what belongs to me. But I keep her on the edge, running my finger in lazy circles around her hard clit. Listening to the way her breath grows choppy, and she whimpers my name. Feeling the way she trembles in my arms.

Fucking hell. Just touching her has me dancing the razor's edge. My balls are so full they hurt. My cock is so hard he's in danger of snapping in half.

She hasn't even touched me, and I'm in danger of coming all over myself.

What is she doing to me? Better question, how the fuck do I convince her to keep doing it for the rest of my life?

I circle her tight little hole, driving us both crazy. Beads of sweat roll down my back. Every muscle in my body is locked tight, trying to keep me from picking her gorgeous ass up over my shoulder, finding the nearest bedroom, and railing her until she's screaming the fucking roof down around us.

"You like that, lamb?" I ask, my voice a gritty rasp of sound as I slowly press one thick finger inside of her. She writhes against the door, babbling quiet pleas. "Do you like knowing even part of me is inside you right now?"

"Yes," she gasps. "Please, Zayne."

"Please, what, lamb?"

"Please."

"Tell me what you want, and I'll give it to you."

"I...I..."

"Say the words, Emma. Tell me that you want me to make you come all over me."

She's said it about a thousand times in my dreams, but I want to hear it in reality. No, I *need* to hear that sweet voice pleading with me to make her come on me. I'm going to lose my mind if I don't hear it soon.

"Please," she begs.

"No, Emma. Say the words."

"Please make me come all over you, Zayne," she whispers in desperation. "*Please*."

I groan, burying my face in her throat as I set to work, giving her exactly what she asked for so sweetly. I set my thumb against her clit, grinding in firm circles as I curl my finger up, looking for her sweet spot.

I know the instant I find it.

A startled cry of ecstasy leaves her lips, and her inner muscles flutter wildly. She shakes in my arms as she falls to pieces, her sticky juices making a fucking mess of my hand.

I work her through it, not letting up until she goes limp in my arms, panting for breath. Once she does, I peel her away from the door, holding her to my chest.

"Did that feel as good as it sounded?"

"Yes," she whispers shyly.

"Good." I press my lips to her temple, breathing her in. "Next time, you'll be doing it on my tongue."

"N-next time?"

"Oh, lamb," I laugh quietly. "You never should have let me through the front door. Because now that I'm here, I have no intentions of leaving until every piece of you belongs to me." I tip her chin up, planting a kiss on her lips. "Starting with your heart."

"Zayne."

"Come on. We should get out of here before Gran and Bets come looking and realize what we've been doing in here."

"Zayne!"

I ignore her, knowing damn well she's trying to talk herself out of falling for me. It's too late for that, though. She never would have let me in if she wasn't already halfway there. We both know she knows this whole bodyguard story is bullshit. But she let me sell it anyway.

She's falling in love with me.

And I fully intend to be here to catch her when she makes the final swan dive off the edge.

Chapter Eight

EMMA

"Gran, we're not sleeping together," I growl, throwing my hands up as Gran tries to convince me for the fifth time to let Zayne sleep in the room with me. "Aren't you supposed to be telling me that I should save myself for marriage instead of trying to throw me at Zayne?"

"Save yourself for marriage?" Gran eyes me like I've lost my mind. "I'm old, not dead, Emmaline. I saw the way that sweet boy was looking at you through dinner. Whether he's in your bed tonight or after he has a ring on your finger, he'll be putting a ring on your finger."

I groan, flopping down on my bed to stare up at the ceiling. "I'm surrounded by crazy people," I mutter to the spackling. "Somehow, I'm the sanest person in this house."

"Not if you're making that boy sleep on the couch, you're not," Gran snorts, perching on the bed beside me.

I turn my head to glare at her, which only makes her laugh at me. "You can pout about it all you want, but tantrums never changed the truth, girl. That boy is in love with you."

"Zayne outgrew being called a boy about two decades and ten inches ago, Gran."

"When you're my age, no one is too big to be considered a boy. Stop trying to change the subject. That boy is in love with you."

She's right. Zayne Carmichael is in love with me. Even worse, I think he's in love with Gran and Bets. Every defense I had against him is rapidly dissolving. And I've never been more terrified in my life.

I thought if I kept him at a distance, I'd protect my heart, but after watching him with Gran and Bets tonight, I realized my mistake.

There's no defense against the inevitable. I've been falling since day one. Even when I fought it. Even when I denied it. Even when I pretended it wasn't happening, I was falling. I think I crash-landed sometime today.

I don't even know when, either! But my heart is in his hands, and that's not even the terrifying part. The part that really scares me is the fact that I don't know the first thing about being in love. What if I mess it up? What if I'm just not good at it?

What if I break him?

"I don't want to break him, Gran," I admit in a whisper.

"What makes you think you will?"

I shrug helplessly, not sure I know how to put into words why I've been fighting him so hard.

"Your mama," Gran guesses.

Tears immediately spring to my eyes. "She broke everyone she was supposed to love."

"That's because your mama was an addict, sweet girl. Addiction breaks everything." Gran slips her frail hand into mine, squeezing. For some reason, even though she broke my dad's heart and eventually got them both killed, Gran has never hated my mom. She's never had anything bad to say about her.

My dad caught her in bed with another man when I was just a little girl. It broke him. He kicked her out, but he never got over her. Less than a year later, she came around asking for help like she did from time to time. He couldn't tell her no. He never was able to tell her no.

He took her to pay off her dealer...and her dealer killed both of them. My dad never should have been there, but he just couldn't stop trying to rescue her. He packed all my stuff up that morning before he left, as if he knew he wouldn't be coming home that night.

What my mom's dealer did wasn't my mom's fault. He made his own choice, one that he didn't have to make. But part of me blames her anyway. Because of her choices, I grew up without my parents.

I think I've spent most of my life afraid I'd end up like her...selfishly destroying the people I love. Hiding behind caring for Gran and Bets has made it easy to keep from facing that. So long as I had them to worry about, I had an excuse to keep everyone else at a distance. But Zayne's here now, and I'm tottering on the edge of something terrifying.

What if I mess it up? What if I break him like my mom broke my dad? What if I destroy his life like her addiction destroyed all of ours? They weren't perfect lives by any means, but at least I had parents, Gran had her son, and we had each other.

Now, all I have is Gran and Bets. And I'm all they have, too.

"I don't want to hurt him," I whisper.

"Then put your big girl panties on and stop running, sweet girl. Because even if he never says it, that's what will hurt him. He needs you to trust yourself and trust him. That's how you love him, with your whole heart. Just like you do everything else. If you do that, the rest will fall into place." Gran presses her lips to my cheek. "I'm getting in bed. I might even take my sleeping medication tonight so I sleep as hard as Bets does."

"Gran," I groan. "I already told you that we aren't sleeping together."

She winks at me before hauling herself up from the bed. "Then that's a crying shame, Emmaline Cooper. That man was made for long nights and sturdy headboards."

"You did not just say that."

She shrugs, as unrepentant as ever. "Live a little. God knows, I'm not getting any younger. If you're going to give me great-grandbabies, you'd better do it soon."

"Gran!" I hiss.

"I'm just saying, we've brought you enough of those smutty books to have taught you a thing or two by now. You ought to be able to figure out how it works."

"Oh, my God," I laugh through a groan. "I don't know if you believe half the stuff you say or if you say it just to watch me squirm."

"I'll never tell, dear," she sing-songs as she sails out of the room. "Goodnight!"

"Night, Gran. Love you."

"Love you too."

Half an hour later, a soft rap on the door sends my heart into overdrive. I don't even have to ask to know it's Zayne. I don't have to guess to know what will happen if I let him in.

The only thing standing between me and him is one door and about fifteen years of family trauma. But not even that sounds so loud in the dead of night. Or maybe talking to Gran helped. I don't know.

All I know for sure is that the only man who has ever made me want to risk it is standing on the other side of the door, waiting for me to decide if I want to let him in...and I don't want to spend the rest of my life afraid to actually live it.

I don't want to wake up fifty years from now, wondering if I let the best thing that ever happened to me slip through my fingers. Maybe I am like my mom, destined to hurt the people I love. Maybe I'm like my dad, destined to spend my life flutily trying to put back together the pieces of a broken heart. Maybe I'll be like Gran, spinning like a top without the man of my dreams to ground me. Or maybe I'm meant to take all of those fears and niggling worries and doubts and forge them into my own destiny. I don't know. I don't have all the answers.

But I do have this one.

I scurry across the room, pulling the door open.

Zayne's gray eyes slide down my body, doing a slow perusal. "Only you could make cat pajamas sexy, lamb."

"Hi," I whisper.

He lifts his gaze to mine. "You okay? I could hear you overthinking from the living room."

"Sorry." I grimace. "I mean, no, you couldn't."

"So you were overthinking."

"Yes. No." I huff, crossing my arms to glare at him. "Stop confusing me."

He chuckles, one side of his mouth quirking up into a sexy smile. "Stop being so fuckin' cute."

"I can't help the way God made me, Zayne."

His smile grows as he glances over my head. "Your room is nice. Doesn't match the rest of the house."

"You mean it doesn't look like we robbed a furniture store?" My room is the only one in the house where everything matches. Every other room is a treasure trove of antiques and flea market finds Gran and Bets just had to have. At least until they find the perfect piece to replace it. Redecorating makes them happy, so I don't complain.

"That's one way to put it."

I laugh quietly. "Gran and Bets like to shop. They're forever swapping out one piece of furniture or another. I put my foot down about changing things in here after I woke up to find a four-foot giraffe standing in the corner."

I nearly fell out of my bed. Gran thought I'd get a kick out of the wooden sculpture. I'm still not entirely sure how they hauled it in here by themselves. It was heavy!

"They're wild, aren't they?"

"You don't know the half of it," I mutter. "My grandpa died six years ago. He was the only thing keeping them in line."

"You've been carin' for them since you were seventeen?"

"For the most part. Gran had a stroke a year after Grandpa died. Her judgment hasn't been the best since then. I'm not sure Bets ever had good judgment. Individually, they're manageable, but together?" I tuck strands of hair behind my ears, shaking my head. "Well, let's just say it's a miracle neither of them has ended up in jail for very long."

"For very long?" His right brow climbs.

"I told you that they're wild." I stare at him with wide eyes. "Do you have any idea how hard it is to convince a judge that your seventy-seven-year-old aunt didn't mean to flee from the police when you're pretty sure she actually did mean to do it?"

"Jesus Christ," he laughs in disbelief.

I'm not making it up, though. With them, I'm never making it up. When Grandpa was still here, he could talk them down or at least mitigate some of the damage. But without him, they don't even try to behave. It's like they've decided they're done playing by the rules and are going to spend their last years living life on their terms. I don't begrudge them that. I love them for it. But that doesn't mean I don't worry.

"They adore you."

"The feeling is mutual. I wouldn't change them," I whisper fiercely. "Not even for a second."

"But you worry," he says.

"So much. I live in a constant state of anxiety, afraid one of them will go too far and they'll end up hurt or worse. I'm not ready to live my life without them because I wasn't watching closely enough.".

"That's not going to happen, lamb." Zayne reaches for me, tugging me into his arms. "I'll make sure of it."

"That's not your job."

"Taking care of you is my job."

My stomach churns with anxiety. "We both know you aren't really here because I'm in danger, Zayne. I just...I don't understand why you're here at all," I admit. "Why are you so willing to jump headfirst into all of this?"

"You might not be in physical danger, but that doesn't mean you don't need me, Emma." He tips my chin up until our eyes meet. "It doesn't mean you aren't in danger at all."

"I'm not."

"You're in danger of sacrificing more than you can afford to give, lamb. You're so busy takin' care of everyone else, but no one has been taking care of you."

"I take care of me."

"Now, you don't have to do it. You have me."

"But why?" I blurt.

"You really don't know?" He cups my cheek, rubbing his thumb along my jaw. "You really can't see it?"

"I..." I swallow hard, my stomach churning with anxiety. "I see it," I finally manage to whisper. "I think that's exactly why I've been fighting this so hard, Zayne."

"Why?"

"What if...what if I'm not good at this?" I ask. "What if I mess it all up and ruin your life?"

"You really think you could do that?"

I lick my lips, trying to find the words. I've never told anyone about my parents, not even Camila. "My mom was an addict. She hurt a lot of people. I think she hurt my dad worst of all. He was crazy about her, but you can't love an addiction out of someone. He found that out the hard way."

"Damn," Zayne whispers, pulling me closer, as if he can physically protect me from my past and the memories of it.

"Her dealer ended up killing them both."

"How old were you?"

"Nine."

"Jesus."

"The saddest part is that I think he knew what was going to happen. My dad, I mean. Before he left to go meet her dealer that day to pay him off, he packed up all of my stuff. I remember him sending me off to school that morning, hugging me like it was the last time he was going to see me." A few hours later, he and my mom were dead. I *still* think about the way he hugged me that morning.

"You think he knew he was going to die?"

"I think he knew it was a possibility. But he loved my mom, so he went anyway. Part of me thinks maybe he hoped it'd end that way just so he didn't have to keep living without her." I take a breath. "I'm not sure if I'm more afraid of you breaking my heart or if I'm more afraid that I'll end up breaking yours."

"You think I could break your heart, lamb?"

"I think you're the only man I've ever met who has the power to break it," I admit, giving him the truth I've been trying so hard to fight. The one that seals my fate, and perhaps his too.

I'm in love with this man. For better or worse, he has my heart. I just hope he knows what to do with it because I don't have a clue.

Chapter Nine

ZAYNE

I stare at Emma, trying to process. Is she saying she's in love with me? I'm afraid to hope, but I hope anyway. It's a powerful thing when it's all you've got.

"Why are you so sure I'll break your heart, baby girl?"

"I don't know." She shrugs helplessly. "Maybe because you make me feel something I'm afraid to lose."

"What's that?"

"Like I'm not alone." Her earnest, fearful expression cracks my heart in half. She's carried a helluva lot for a helluva long time, more than anyone should have had to carry. Fears about turning out like her mom, grief over losing her parents, and responsibility for Gran and Bets...she had to grow up way too fucking fast. That kills me for her.

"I've been responsible for everything for so freaking long, Zayne. Carrying it all is exhausting. And then you come along and promise me that I'm safe. You make me feel like maybe I could lean on you, but I've never had that. I don't want to lose it, and I'm terrified if I let you get any closer, I will."

"Fuck," I growl. Of course, she's scared she's going to lose it. She's lost more than anyone should, far before she ever should have. Of course, she's afraid to let me in when it means opening herself to the possibility that she could lose more. But she's worked herself into knots over nothing.

I'm not going anywhere. There's not a damn thing she could do that would change my mind. Even on her worst day, she isn't capable of inflicting the kind of damage her mother inflicted. That's simply not who she is. She's bright and shining and pure, all the way down to her foundation.

And I'll work my ass off to guard that part of her, to protect it like the treasure it is. That's my job as her man. To let the world harden me so she stays soft and sweet. To use my back as a shield so nothing ever touches her.

I fucking hate that she's spent so much of her life afraid she'll end up alone, but hell will freeze over before I let that happen.

"You aren't going to lose it, Emma," I murmur. "I'm not goin' anywhere. And I don't give a shit what Gran and Bets do. I've been to hell and back for this country. You think I wouldn't do the same for you and those two old ladies to keep the three of you together?"

"It's not fair to ask you to help me with them, Zayne."

"You aren't asking, lamb. I'm telling you this is how it's going to be," I say, making the choice for her. "You wobbled your gorgeous ass into my office and stole my heart. Whether you want it or not, it's yours. So you might as well get used to the idea of me sticking around. You might as well prepare yourself for the fact that I'm going to be here, driving you just as fucking crazy as they do."

I release her, taking a step back to unbutton my shirt.

"What are you doing?" she asks warily.

"Showing you something." I quickly work the buttons through the holes before slipping the shirt off my shoulders and tossing it over the end of her bed. Her eyes eat me up, making my cock throb. But I ignore the greedy bastard for a moment, reaching for her hand. "Do you know what this means, baby girl?"

She traces her fingers over the tattoo on my chest, her touch searing me. "*Familia ante omnia*," she murmurs, reading the script inked there. "Familia means family, but I don't know the rest."

"It says *family over all*. It means family comes before everything." I tug her back into my arms, tipping her head back until those pretty blue eyes are locked on my face again. "They aren't just words inked into my skin. They're precisely the way I've always lived my life. My family comes before everything else."

"I love that," she whispers.

"You're family now, lamb. Gran and Bets are family now."

"Zayne." Her expression goes soft as her fingers dance over the delicate lines of ink.

"I'm in love with you, Emmaline Cooper. Madly, wildly, crazily in love with your gorgeous ass. So I'm going to need you to be brave and trust that I'm not going anywhere. Not today or tomorrow or the first time Gran and Bets cause a problem. Not the fifteenth or fiftieth time, either. You're family, and I don't give up on my family."

She blinks up at me, awe stamped across every delicate line of her face. "You mean that, don't you?"

"Which part?"

"All of it."

"Every word." I brush my lips across hers.

"I love you too," she whispers.

For the first time in my life, I know what perfection feels like. And for the first time in my life, I know exactly what heaven looks like. It's this curvy little lamb staring up at me with desire in her eyes and love on her lips.

"You can't take it back now, Emma," I warn her. "Not the words, not your heart, not any of it. You're mine now."

"I think I've always been yours, Zayne." Her gaze flickers over my face. "At least, I have been since I met you. Maybe even before. You feel inevitable, like fate."

"Fuck," I growl, claiming her lips. I pour my fucking soul into it as she slips into place in mine, lighting it up like a brand on flesh. Only, there is no pain. There's just pure fucking rapture.

She kisses me back just as deeply, her tongue working with mine as if she intends to live off the taste of me. I'll let her. Christ, I think I'd sell my soul at this point to keep this woman kissing me exactly like she can't get enough.

She mewls, coming back for more again and then again...just like I did in the bathroom earlier. It's as if she's as helpless to stop herself as I was. She does nothing in half measures. When she fights, she fights for all she's worth. And when she surrenders, she surrenders every little piece of herself.

They're all mine now to worship however the fuck I want. I might just start on my knees where a motherfucker belongs. At least that's the plan until she slips her hand between us, running it across my pecs and then down my abdomen, bolder than she's ever been.

My entire body reacts to her touch. I tremble at the feel of her skin against mine. My dick throbs, begging her to continue her little exploration a little further south.

She keeps them above my waist, though, slowly driving me out of my mind. Right up until I boost her up in arms, trying to get some part of her where I want her.

Her legs encircle my waist, giving me a little taste of heaven as her pussy settles against my cock. Christ Almighty. If I'm not claiming her cherry and her womb soon, I'm going to snap.

"Oh," she gasps when she feels how fucking hard I am.

I wrap my hands around her, meaning to anchor her in place while I deal with the door. But Gran and Bets aren't the only two around here who don't know how to behave. Something flares in her eyes as she shifts around, wriggling against my cock.

"Fuck, that feels exactly like heaven."

She digs her nails into my shoulders and does it again.

I have her pressed against the door in two seconds, dry-humping her like my goddamn life depends on it. "Keep playing with me, and you'll be on your back, screaming my name before you can blink, lamb," I snarl, grinding my dick against her hot little center again.

"Who says I'm playing, Zayne?" she whispers back. Her nails rake down my arms, sending a bolt of desire right to my cock. "Maybe that's exactly what I want."

I buck my hips, growling. "You want me to fuck you through the mattress? Because that's what's going to happen if you don't behave. It's been a helluva long month."

"I just want you. However I can get you, Zayne. It's been a long month for me, too."

That's all I need to hear. Her every whim is my command.

I tear her thin pajama top down the middle, groaning when the fabric parts.

"Jesus Christ. Look at these." I bury my face between her tits. Who could resist? They're right there, looking like they were made for my mouth.

Her hand flies to my hair, holding me to her when I turn my head to the side, allowing me to drag one hard nipple into my mouth. She tastes exactly like she smells...like fucking sunshine and magic.

I lavish attention on her tits, moving from one to the other until they're red with my marks, and she's writhing all over my cock, pleading for release.

"Are we movin' fast enough for you now, lamb?" I ask, peeling her away from the door to drop her on her bed. She bounces before sinking into the plush surface.

"N-no."

No?

Fuck. She has no sense of self-preservation at all. She's waving herself in front of a starving beast, curious to see if he'll take a bite. I have news for her. I may not be causing chaos like Gran and Bets, but I'm far from tame. If she wants me wild, that's exactly what she's going to get.

I pop the button on my slacks before crawling onto the bed over her. She stares up at me with those blue eyes that see straight to my soul, her cheeks flushed with desire.

"You're the sweetest little lamb I've ever met, Emma," I mutter, leaning down to brush a kiss against her mouth. "If you don't stop fucking with me, I'm going to teach you what lions do to lambs."

"Show me."

I growl, hooking my arm around her waist to haul her toward the center of the bed. She splays out in the middle of it, her arms flung wide as if she's inviting me to do my worst. If we're going to be staying here instead of at my place, we're going to need a bigger bed. Hers is too fucking small for all the ways I intend to put it to use.

"Stop me now if you don't plan to be carrying my kid before the end of the night."

"You want babies with me?" She smiles, her expression soft and sweet.

"Want them?" I snort derisively. "You'll be lucky if I don't keep you pregnant for the next ten years."

"I always wanted a big family," she whispers.

Well, shit, I guess I better get my ass to work then.

I brush another kiss across her lips before kissing my way down her body, stripping her shorts and panties from her in the process. Not a single inch of skin is left unexplored as I journey toward her juicy cunt. A spurt of cum shoots into my boxers when I'm face to face with that holy place, her legs splayed wide.

Her lips are spread open, her hard clit peeping from between them. Honey drips all the way down the crevice of her luscious ass, wetting her thick thighs.

"So fuckin' perfect," I groan, pressing a reverent kiss to her mound. She startles slightly and then moans. I shoulder her legs as far apart as I can get them, lifting her toward my mouth. My tongue runs along her lips, collecting her juices. As soon as they touch my tongue, I lose my fucking mind, exactly like I knew I would.

I attack her cunt like an unruly beast, not being polite about it.

She cries out, shock and ecstasy ringing around us as she grabs chunks of my hair. I use my teeth and tongue to drive her wild, not missing a single drop of the honey flowing from her. Her taste floods my mouth, and short-circuits my system. It still isn't enough.

I flip her onto her stomach, lifting her ass in the air to eat her from behind.

"Zayne!" she cries out, shocked when I pry her cheeks apart to shove my tongue between them. She chokes on a sob when I press the tip of it to her little asshole, taking everything that belongs to me like the greedy motherfucker I am. If she wanted soft and sweet, she shouldn't have played with fire.

Because I intend to burn the fucking bed down around us.

My hand comes down on her right cheek, as I bite the left, marking her there. Her startled yelp fades to a moan. She presses back for more, practically waving that ass in my face. I give her what she wants, eating both holes while I swat her cheeks. I smack her clit, too, fucking loving the way she sobs my name every time I do it. Loving the wet sound of my hand meeting her soppy pussy.

Her juices drip onto my chest, coating me in her, and still, I want more. I need it more than I need air or water or shelter. This right here is what I was made to do: spend my time on my knees, worshipping like an obedient little soldier. For her, that's precisely what I am. I may make the rules, but she holds all the power. She has since the moment I set eyes on her.

"Goddamn," I growl. "Lamb just because my favorite meal. I could eat you all night, Emma." I pull her clit into my mouth, sucking hard. "Maybe that's exactly what I'll do. Eat you all night." I stiffen my tongue, forcing the tip of it into her little hole. I want to taste the cherry on her. I fuck her with my tongue, giving her a little preview of what's to come.

"Zayne! Oh, God. What are you doing to me?"

Ruining you, I want to say, but I'm not stopping long enough to do that.

I smack her ass again, reaching around to grind my thumb against her clit at the same time.

She comes with a sharp cry, squirting all over me. I snarl against her pussy, losing what little sanity I had left. Before she's even finished shaking, I've got my dick out and have her on her back beneath me, pinning her to the bed with my body.

"Next time you do that, it'll be while I'm fucking my kid into you," I warn her.

"Yes. Please, yes." Her pupils are so dilated her eyes look black as she stares up at me, whimpering my name like it's the only one she knows. She locks her legs around my waist, letting me know just how much she likes my plan.

My cock glides through her sticky folds, her juices coating me. The heat of her sets every nerve ending in my body to firing at once.

Christ Almighty. I think I might actually be in danger of fucking her through the mattress here.

"I don't know how to be gentle," I say, distressed at the thought of hurting her. I'm so fucking amped up, I'm not sure I know how to be soft and sweet and give her what she deserves. But I'll rip my own goddamn heart out before I cause her the least amount of pain.

"You won't hurt me," she says, reaching up to place her palm against my cheek. The confidence in her gaze strengthens my own. "I can take anything you give me, so give it to me, Zayne. Make me yours."

A bolt of lust rips through me. I line up at her entrance, planting my lips beside her ear. "Give me what belongs to me, lamb."

"Take it," she breathes, her nails in my back.

I bury my face in her throat, fighting a roar as I thrust forward. I try to tell her that I love her, but all that comes out is, "Ah, Jesus fuck, baby girl."

I'm barely in her, and she's already got me hanging on by a thread. Her heels dig into my ass, her upper body arching off the bed. She writhes, caught in a net of pleasure and pain.

One minute, she's sobbing my name and clawing down my back, trying to pull me closer. The next, her hymen tears along the side of my shaft. Her teeth sink into my skin, muffling her soft cry.

I fall completely still, trying to give her a minute to adjust.

"Please, please," she chants. "Oh, God, Zayne."

"Breathe, lamb," I rasp. "Just breathe for me."

"I didn't k-know."

"Know what?"

"That it'd feel like this," she cries.

I lift my head to look at her. Only then do I realize she's not writhing in pain but in ecstasy. I just popped her cherry, and she loved every second of it.

I slip forward another inch. Her pussy clenches around my cock, another flood of honey spilling across my shaft.

"Jesus," I growl, the evidence of her pleasure snapping the bonds of my self-control. She can handle me. Fuck, I think she may *own* me.

I stop worrying about hurting her and start moving.

I surge forward and fall back, pounding into her as if I intend to imprint my cock inside her. Hell, maybe that's exactly what I mean to do. Ensure she remembers I was here even when I'm not. Aches for me as soon as I'm gone. *Lives* for this.

"So good, so good," she babbles, clawing my back all to hell.

I tip my head down, claiming her mouth in a punishing kiss. Her mouth moves with mine. She moves with me, meeting every stroke, matching my rhythm. If I was born to worship her, she was born to let me do it with her on my cock. She bites and scratches, leaving her marks littering my body.

I leave mine behind too, creating a roadmap of love bites across her skin. The hollow of her throat. Her breasts. Her right shoulder. Everywhere I can reach as I drive into her, lost in her and the powerful blasts of pleasure threatening to annihilate me.

I want to possess her, bury myself in her so deeply she can't ever get me out again.

That's my new goal in life. To spend the rest of it fucking her just like this. To spend it tying her soul to mine so tightly, I'll find her in whatever life comes next. Because now that I've had a taste of this? Now that I know she exists, and this is what we are together? There's not a single version of eternity that interests me unless I get to spend it exactly like this.

She's mine. *Mine. Mine. Mine.*

"Yes," she sobs. "Yes, I'm yours."

Only then do I realize I'm saying it out loud, growling the word *mine* every time I thrust into her. Her agreement fans the flames, sending me higher. I fuck her harder, deeper. Until I can't fight it anymore.

If she doesn't come soon, I'm going to explode.

I slip my hand between us, zeroing in on her clit. My teeth sink into the soft skin where her neck meets her shoulder. She practically levitates off the bed, gasping my name. She's right there, toes dangling over the edge.

"I love you."

Those three little words—the simplest truth I've ever spoken—send her free-falling over the side of the cliff. She creams all over my cock, her cunt locking down around my shaft as if she's commanding me to come too.

I go off like a bomb, pumping my cum into her in powerful spurts. I fuck her without rhythm, my hips slamming into hers again and again as I empty myself into her, claiming her womb.

It goes on for an eternity, leaving me blind and shaking. And more convinced than ever that I'll never get enough of this woman. Not today, not tomorrow, and not in this lifetime or any that comes after it.

I'm hers, permanently, unalterably. Forever.

Chapter Ten

EMMA

"Tell me something."

"What do you want to know?" Zayne asks.

"Anything."

His slow grin heats my blood to boiling. Lord, he's gorgeous, especially when the only thing he's wearing is a carefully arranged sheet. I'll never tell Bets, but this sight is definitely worthy of a book cover.

"You want me to tell you how good you sound when you're moanin' my name?" he asks, gliding one hand up my side. "Or would you rather hear how fucking hot you are when you're coming all over me?"

"I meant, tell me something about you, Zayne," I say, rolling my eyes at him. I can't fight a smile, though. If this is what heaven is like, I definitely need to go there.

"Something about me, huh?" He taps his lip like he's thinking. And then he grins. "You want to know a secret?"

"I'm a girl. We always want to know secrets."

"Come here, and I'll tell you." He hooks his arm around my waist, hauling me into his arms. Once I'm where he wants me, which is apparently sprawled across his chest, he brushes my hair aside, putting his lips against my ear.

"You weren't the only virgin in this bed tonight, lamb."

I scramble up, staring at him in shock. "You're lying."

"I'm not."

"You're a virgin?"

He casts a wicked glance down my naked body. "Not anymore," he says, deadpan.

"Zayne!" I smack him across the chest. "Stop messing with me."

He grabs my hands, holding them hostage in one of his. "I'm not messin' with you, lamb. You're my first and only, too."

"I..." My mind spins. "You're serious."

"Yep."

I stare at him for a moment, truly at a loss for words. I never even considered that tonight was the first time for him, too. I guess I just assumed that he's had plenty of chances, so he had to have taken at least a few of them. But Zayne isn't like anyone I've ever known before. He's just Zayne.

I didn't stand a chance of not falling for him.

"Were you saving for marriage?" I ask.

He makes a face at me. "No, smartass. I was saving myself for you."

"Zayne," I whisper, my expression going soft as my heart flutters.

"I've spent my entire fucking life preparing for you, lamb. I just didn't know it until the day you wobbled into my office." He grins at me. "Now, you're here, and it all makes sense."

"What does?"

"Everything." He rolls me underneath him, nuzzling my throat. "This right here is what I've been waiting for my whole life."

I swallow hard. "I'm done keeping you waiting."

"Yeah?"

"Yeah," I whisper. "I'm so done."

"Good," he grunts, hooking my leg over his hip. "Because I've got a whole lotta time to make up for now that I've got you where I want you."

"You mean naked in my bed with my grandma and aunt right down the hall?"

"Pretty much," he breathes.

My laugh fades to a moan as he gets busy making up for lost time. For a recent virgin, he's awful good at it.

"What is that sound?" I grumble, trying to bury myself under the blankets as if that'll make it quit. But whatever it is, it's not that easily deterred. Even with the blankets over my head, it continues blaring as if trying to warn me that a catastrophe is imminent.

Warn me?

I fly upright on a gasp, flinging the covers back. It is trying to warn me that a catastrophe is imminent. It's the security system I had installed after Gran and Bets ran off to Tunica.

I don't bother getting dressed or explaining the situation to Zayne. I simply grab my robe from the back of the door, shove my arms through it, and dash out into the hall, hoping I make it in time to stop whatever they're plotting this time.

I skid around the corner into the living room just in time to see the front door close. Except Gran and Bets aren't on the other side of it. They're standing in the center of the room, removing their coats as if they just got home.

Zayne isn't in the bed where I left him...or thought I left him, anyway. He's coming through the door, chuckling at something. He crosses to the security system, punching in the code.

Silence rings throughout the house, infinitely louder than the alarm.

"What is this?" I blurt, trying to figure out if I'm even awake or not. Gran and Bets haven't escaped, and the man of my dreams is still here, looking even better than he did on top of me a few short hours ago.

My cheeks heat at the reminder that he was on top of me a few short hours ago. Neither of us slept very much. We spent the night alternately making love and talking. It was, hands down, the best night of my life.

I'm done running, and I'm over fighting to resist him. I'm all in, no matter where it leads. I choose him. How could I not when he's everything I ever dreamed about?

"Shit," he growls, his eyes coming to me. His expression goes soft, those gray eyes eating me alive. "We woke you."

"Good morning, dear!" Gran says cheerfully.

"I was beginning to wonder if you were getting up today," Bets says.

"What's going on?"

"We went shopping." Zayne hefts the shopping bags I somehow missed. He's loaded down with them.

"You went shopping?" I ask, trying to process again.

"Mmhmm. Gran needed supplies." He strides across the room, brushing his lips across mine as if we're completely alone. Heat unfurls in my stomach, rippling outward in a slow flood.

Jeez. How is it possible that I want him again already? Every muscle in my body is deliciously sore from last night.

"For what?"

"Your wedding dress, dear. It's not going to sew itself."

"I'm making your cake," Bets adds.

Dress? Cake? I gape, convinced I'm still in bed dreaming.

Gran sees the look on my face and grins, one of those bawdy, mischievous grins that guarantee I'm going to regret whatever comes out of her mouth.

I'm not wrong.

"You can't be making all that racket you were making last night if you aren't charried to the boy, dear. It's unseemly."

I blanche as Zayne barely contains a laugh.

"Gran!"

"I'm just saying. It may be a new millennium, but times haven't changed that much," she says.

"Marriage before babies, Emma. Marriage before babies."

Zayne isn't even trying to hide his laughter now.

"I'm going back to bed," I say weakly.

"No can do." Zayne snags me around the waist before I can make an escape. "Unless you intend to drag everyone down to the courthouse, you've got a weddin' to plan."

"What?" I gape at him. "You aren't serious." Except...I can already tell that he's completely serious. This crazy man fully intends to marry me immediately.

I glance at Gran and Bets, just to find them beaming at us. They're fully on board with this plan.

"How did I become the lone voice of reason in this house?" I mumble up at the ceiling.

"Because you're dramatic, dear," Gran says. "Just tell the boy yes and get on with it already."

"You're supposed to talk me out of rushing into things."

"I'm eighty, Emmaline. The only way to do things at my age is in a hurry. Otherwise, you're liable to wake up dead."

"You can't wake up dead, Gran."

"Oh? Are you an expert then?"

Zayne chuckles.

"Don't encourage her."

"She has a point," he says with a shrug.

"You're only agreeing with her because she's taking your side."

"Maybe, but that doesn't negate the fact that she has a point." He smirks at me. "Stop overthinking and start plannin' your dream wedding, lamb. My rules, remember?"

"Your rules didn't say anything about me marrying you, Zayne Carmichael!"

"It was in the fine print."

"You always read the fine print, girl," Bets cackles.

"Are you really going to fight me on this, baby girl? We both know you want it as much as I do," Zayne murmurs. "You wouldn't have let me lie my way through your front door if you didn't."

I cast a furtive glance at Gran and Bets.

"We're old, not stupid, Emmaline. The only thing that boy is protecting you from is anyone trying to steal you out from under him."

"At least I don't have to worry about either of you trying to buy a gun to protect the house," I mutter, relieved we're not pretending anymore. I don't think either of us was very good at it. But we were both willing to do it anyway. Maybe Gran and Bets aren't the only crazy ones in this room.

"Why in the world would I need to buy a gun?" Gran asks. "I already have one in the closet."

"You don't," I groan.

"Of course, I do. You think the only thing your grandpa left me was money?" She tsks at me, her poufy hair bouncing with the force of her head shake. "You should know better than that, Emmaline. Really."

"Do you know how to shoot it?" Zayne asks, finally worried about something. It's about time! I mean, honestly.

"Not a clue," Gran says cheerfully. "But I've got a box of bullets and know where to put them. I also know where the business end of the thing is located. I can figure it out from there."

Zayne pales slightly. "Maybe I should hold onto the gun."

Gran shrugs like it doesn't matter one way or another who has the gun so long as it shoots.

"Are we planning this wedding or not?" Bets wants to know.

All eyes turn in my direction, patiently waiting for my answer.

"You didn't ask me," I hiss at Zayne.

"Is that why you're dragging your feet saying yes?"

"I can't say yes if there isn't a question, Zayne Carmichael."

"In that case..." He drops to his knees right there in the middle of the floor, one arm still loaded with shopping bags. He carefully sets them aside before reaching into his pocket to retrieve something.

Tears well in my eyes when he holds his hand out, and I spot the ring resting in his palm.

"You gave him your ring," I whisper to Gran.

"Of course I did. It's been yours since your grandpa died. I've just been waiting for you to find the man worthy of you. Now that you have, it's time for that old ring to be shining on your finger where it belongs."

I sniffle, trying—and failing—to fight tears. She's giving me her ring, and she thinks Zayne is worthy of me. Her judgment may be faulty most days, but it's impeccable today. There is no one more worthy of me. I don't think there ever will be.

This crazy man is it for me...and that's not nearly as terrifying as I let myself believe it was. For the first time, I realize it's not terrifying at all. In fact, it's the complete opposite. Nothing would make me happier than spending the rest of my life loving this crazy man.

"Zayne?"

"Yes, lamb?"

"I have to fire you as my bodyguard."

He cocks his head to the side, eyeing me curiously. "Why is that, lamb?"

"Apparently, I have a sudden opening for a fiancé. I was kind of hoping you'd want to fill that position instead."

His smile is bright enough to light up the entire room. "Oh, yeah?" He grabs my hand, slipping Gran's ring into place on my finger. "I think I can make that happen."

"Are you sure? I hear the wedding is soon."

"Real soon," he growls, rising to his feet with fire in his eyes. "As soon as humanly possible."

"Yeah? You sure you're available?" I tease. "Maybe we should check and make sure I don't need to ask your broth—"

I squeal with laughter as he scoops me up into his arms.

"Finish that sentence, and I'll be spanking you right here in front of Gran and Bets," he growls, earning cackles from both of them. His lips slant down over mine, stealing my laughter and my breath.

I cling to his broad shoulders, happy, in love...and surrounded by the best kind of crazy. The kind steeped in love and forged within the bonds of family.

Epilogue

ZAYNE

<u>Five Years Later</u>

"Zayne," Emma moans, rolling her hips as she drops down on my cock, taking me to the hilt. I grunt, wrapping her hair around my fist before gently using my hold on her to drag her down to my mouth.

"I told you to be quiet," I growl, biting her bottom lip. "If you wake them up before I'm finished with you, you'll pay for it later."

She moans again, louder this time. She's playing with fire, trying to get herself burned. It's her favorite pastime. If I tell her not to do something, she goes out of her way to do it. That shouldn't turn me on as much as it does, but it's been five years, and it still gets my cock hard every fucking time she does it.

She knows it, too. She shamelessly uses it to her advantage, leading me around by my cock. I love every second of it. Her brand of magic is still my favorite flavor.

Everyone in our orbit knows it. I make no secret of the fact that I'm obsessed with my wife. I'm a possessive, overprotective motherfucker when it comes to her, and I don't make apologies for it. She's the center of the world. Without her, the whole damn thing falls apart.

My life started making sense the day she wobbled into it in those ridiculous heels. It's made a little more sense every day since. She's the purpose, the passion, the reason. Fuck, she's everything.

"Zayne," she whimpers. "Please."

"Please, what, lamb?"

"Harder."

"Like this?" I lift her, only to yank her back down on my cock.

"Yes!" she cries, her head thrown back.

I do it again and then again, lifting my hips to meet every hard thrust, trying to get as deep as I can. Trying to drive her as wild as she makes me. Jesus Christ, she has no idea what she does to me.

Or maybe she does. I've been telling her for five years. Every filthy thought in my head, I give to her without reservation. I give her the sweet ones, too. They mix with the dirty when she's wrapped around my cock, spilling from my lips in a flood.

I drop her again, grinding the root of my cock against her clit.

Her sweet little gasp lets me know just how close she is. Thank God. My balls can't take much more. She's the sweetest torment every single time.

I slip my hand between us, grinding my thumb against her clit.

"Come, lamb. Before I flip you over and spank your perfect ass while I fuck it."

My threat works as intended. She's a dirty little thing. There isn't a damn thing we haven't done in the last five years...and there isn't a single moment of it she hasn't loved. But when I've got both of her holes stuffed full, and she's wearing my handprints? I think that's her own personal version of heaven.

As soon as I utter the threat, she shatters around me with a sharp cry. I drag her mouth down to mine, trying to silence it before she wakes up trouble.

Her nails rake down my chest, sending me over the edge with her. I hold her down on me, spilling into her...though I know there's not a chance in hell I'm getting her pregnant today.

She's been on birth control since the minute our son was born four years ago. We both thought we wanted to fill the house with babies, but her pregnancy was not easy. Bets got sick halfway through and spent a lot of time in the hospital.

Emma was a nervous wreck. She ended up on bed rest for the last two months of the pregnancy, terrified she was going to go into labor early. She managed to hang on, but it took a miracle. I decided right then and there that we were done. I wasn't willing to put her through that again.

Bets recovered, but caring for her, a newborn, and Gran wasn't easy on her, either. We ended up moving everyone to my place since it's a helluva lot bigger than Gran's little bungalow. The extra space allowed us to hire reinforcements to help take care of Gran and Bets.

Two years ago, they decided they were ready to move into an assisted living facility for good. I guess they'd toyed with the idea before, but it never stuck. Surprisingly, they haven't gotten themselves kicked out yet. It's a miracle, honestly.

They show no signs of slowing anytime soon. They basically terrorize the place. But the staff adores them, and we struck a deal to provide security for the place at a steep discount. It helps smooth over any bumps in the road.

Emma falls across my chest with a sigh, breathing heavily. Little tremors still wrack her body as I wrap my arms around her, holding her close as we come down together.

"Goddamn, baby girl," I growl when we've both caught our breaths. "If I could keep you locked up in this room, existing off my cock, I'd do it."

She moans quietly, which I take for an agreement.

"I love you," I murmur, running my hands down her back.

She lifts her head, giving me that sweet smile. "I love you too, Zayne."

A crash from the other end of the hall has us both whipping our heads toward the bedroom door. I groan, scrubbing a hand down my face.

"Your son and nephew are up," I mutter.

"Uh-huh."

"Why the fuck don't they ever sleep past six? This is cruel and unusual punishment."

"It's your fault."

"How do you figure that?"

"You're the morning person, not me." She shrugs, reluctantly sliding off my lap to snuggle up with my pillow. "Good luck out there."

"I'm not going out there alone, lamb."

"You're the one who told Gideon that we'd keep Cormac this weekend." She pats me on the chest. "That means whatever they're destroying out there is your problem until after nine."

I chuckle, shaking my head at her. "You're lucky I love you, you know that?"

"Yep. But you aren't sweet-talking your way out of this one, Zayne Carmichael. Your son and nephew are lunatics."

"We have your grandma and aunt to thank for that," I remind her. The boys learned everything they know from watching the two of them. I swear to God, they absorbed their bad influence like sponges soaking up water.

"No, I'm pretty sure they got it from you and your brothers. You're all just as bad as Gran and Bets." She yawns, snuggling deeper into the blankets. "You better get out there before they burn the house down. I don't think Kenna and Gideon would appreciate learning their four-year-old committed arson on your watch."

"Jesus Christ. Is that a possibility?"

Emma shrugs. "You guys burned your mom's shed down."

"Zion did that." Shit. Maybe it is a possibility. I hop up from the bed, grabbing a pair of sweats.

Emma's soft laugh chases me as I make a quick dash to the bathroom.

When I come back out, she's rolled up in the blankets like an adorable little burrito. My heart rolls in my chest at the sight. I stride toward her, brushing my lips across her forehead.

"I'm going to get out there and save the house. I'll wake you when it's time to get ready to go see Gran and Bets."

"'Kay," she whispers. "Love you."

"Love you too, lamb." I kiss her again and then head for the door.

"Hey, Zayne?" she calls from behind me.

"Yeah?"

"Best husband ever," she whispers.

I slip out into the hallway, grinning from ear to ear...right up until I see Callum and Cormac trying to wrestle Callum's mattress to the top of the stairs, dressed in bicycle helmets and knee pads, anyway.

Jesus Christ. They're going to try to ride the damn thing down.

Emma's right. She is the sanest person in this house.

Author's Note

Thanks so much for reading! If you enjoyed Zayne and Emma's book, please consider leaving a review!

Zion's story, Madly Yours, is available for pre-order!

Want Callum and Cormac's stories? You can find them in the Silver Spoon Falls universe! The Bodyguard (Cormac's story) is available here. And Callum's Hope (Callum's story) is available here.Gray and Camila's story, Ice Breaker, is also available.

You can also get Adrian and Stella's story, Falling Hard, as a thank you for joining my mailing list!

Follow Nichole

Like free books? Me too! Sign-up for my mailing list at http://authornicholerose.com/newsletter to stay up-to-date on all new releases and for exclusive giveaways and freebies!

Want to connect with me and other readers? Join Nichole Rose's Book Beauties on Facebook!

facebook.com/AuthorNicholeRose/

instagram.com/AuthorNicholeRose

twitter.com/AuthNicholeRose

Carmichael Security Series

The Carmichael brothers have it all: a booming business, brotherhood, and a life of luxury. But these bossy bodyguards don't have time for love until it hits them right in the heart. Too bad their reluctant leading ladies are not on the same page!

It's up to the brothers to convince their curvy soul-mates to give happily-ever-after a chance, and they won't take no for an answer in this laugh-out-loud rom-com series.

Their adventures in love are a steamy blend of humor and heart, proving that when it comes to love, size doesn't matter. Each book in the series explores one brother's journey to love.

Truly Mine (Zayne) http://mybook.to/TrulyMineNR

Madly Hers (Zion) http://mybook.to/MadlyYoursNR

Deeply Yours (Gideon) http://mybook.to/DeeplyHersNR

Silver Spoon Falls Universe

We're taking over the world! Just kidding. We're building our own. Welcome to the Silver Spoon Falls Universe, where forever means exactly that. Our hunky heroes will find their curvy soulmates and a little trouble along the way!

We hope you'll join us this year and next as we introduce you guys to even more of the men and women who call Silver Spoon Falls home in the

Silver Spoon Falls series and the Silver Spoon Underworld series.

Don't worry! We will continue writing our own books too! And these will connect in new and exciting ways to our own worlds, creating one giant book universe for you to explore!

The Silver Spoon Falls Universe:

The Silver Spoon MC: mybook.to/Silver-SpoonMC
The CEO by Loni Ree: mybook.to/TheCEOLoniRee
The Surgeon by Nichole Rose: mybook.to/TheSurgeon
The Cowboy by Loni Ree: mybook.to/TheCowboyLR
The Heir by Nichole Rose: http://mybook.to/TheHeirNR
The Rockstar by Loni Ree: mybook.to/TheRockstarLoniRee
The Lawyer by Nichole Rose: mybook.to/TheLawyerNR
The Architect by Loni Ree: mybook.to/TheArchitectLoniRee
The Prodigy by Nichole Rose: mybook.to/TheProdigyNR
The Prince by Loni Ree: mybook.to/ThePrinceLoniRee

The Bodyguard by Nichole Rose: mybook.to/The
BodyguardNR
Silver Spoon MC Collection: Loni's Crew - mybo
ok.to/SSMCLoniRee
Silver Spoon MC Collection: Nichole's Crew - my
book.to/SSMCNichole

**The Silver Spoon Falls Series: mybook.to/Sil-
verSpoonFalls**
Fischer's Catch by Loni Ree: mybook.to/Fischers
CatchLoniRee
Dillon's Heart by Loni Nichole: mybook.to/Dillon
sHeart
Adam's Fugitive by Loni Ree: mybook.to/AdamsF
ugitiveLoniRee
Razor's Flame by Loni Nichole: mybook.to/Razor
sFlame
Ryker's Reward by Loni Nichole: mybook.to/Ryke
rsReward
Zane's Rebel by Loni Nichole: mybook.to/ZanesR
ebelLoniNichole
Xavier's Kitten by Nichole Rose: mybook.to/Xavi
ersKitten
Callum's Hope by Nichole Rose: mybook.to/Callu
msHope
Grizz's Passion by Loni Nichole: mybook.to/Grizz
Passion

Garrett's Obsession by Loni Nichole: mybook.to/
GarrettsObsession

The Silver Spoon Underworld: mybook.to/SilverSpoonUnderworld
Belle's King by Loni Ree: mybook.to/BellesKingLoniRee
Snow's Prince by Nichole Rose: mybook.to/SnowsPrince
Ariel's Duke by Loni Ree: mybook.to/ArielsDukeLoniRee
Aurora's Knight by Nichole Rose: mybook.to/AurorasKnight

The Silver Spoon Falcons: https://www.amazon.com/dp/B0C6KGFG8H
Allie's Enforcer by Loni Ree:
Leia's Playmaker by Nichole Rose: mybook.to/LeiaFalcons
Carlie's Coach by Loni Ree: mybook.to/AlliesEnforcer
Aspen's Defense by Nichole Rose: mybook.to/AspensDefense
Lana's Winger by Loni Ree: mybook.to/LanasWinger
Gabbi's Goalie by Nichole Rose: mybook.to/GabbisGoalie

Silver Spoon After Dark is also coming in 2023!

Nichole's Book Beauties

Want to connect with Nichole and other readers? We're building a girl gang! Join Nichole Rose's Book Beauties on Facebook for fun, games, and behind-the-scenes exclusives!

Instalove Book Club

The Instalove Book Club is now in session!

Get the inside scoop from your favorite instalove authors, meet new authors to love, and snag a free book and bonus content from featured authors every month. The Instalove Book Club newsletter goes out once per week!

Join the Club: http://instalovebookclub.com

Also by Nichole Rose

<u>Her Alpha Series</u>
Her Alpha Daddy Next Door
Her Alpha Boss Undercover
Her Alpha's Secret Baby
Her Alpha Protector
Her Date with an Alpha
Her Alpha: The Complete Series

<u>Her Bride Series</u>
His Future Bride
His Stolen Bride
His Secret Bride
His Curvy Bride
His Captive Bride
His Blushing Bride
His Bride: The Complete Series

Claimed Series
Possessing Liberty
Teaching Rowan
Claiming Caroline
Kissing Kennedy
Claimed: The Complete Series

Love on the Clock Series
Adore You
Hold You
Keep You
Protect You
Love on the Clock: The Complete Series

The Billionaires' Club
The Billionaire's Big Bold Weakness
The Billionaire's Big Bold Wish
The Billionaire's Big Bold Woman
The Billionaire's Big Bold Wonder
The Billionaires' Club: The Complete Series

Playing for Keeps
Cutie Pie
Ice Breaker

Ice Prince
Ice Giant
Cold as Ice
Ice Storm

Full-Length Titles
Crash into You
Fight for You (coming soon)
Kill for You (coming soon)

The Second Generation
A Blushing Bride for Christmas

Love Bites
Come Undone
Dripping Pearls

Echoes of Forever
His Christmas Miracle
Taken by the Hitman
Wicked Saint

The Ruined Trilogy
Physical Science

Wrecked
Wanton
Wicked
Ruined: The Complete Series

<u>Illicit Love Series</u>
Irresistible
Irrevocable
Irreplaceable
Irredeemable

<u>Destination Romance</u>
Romancing the Cowboy
Beach House Beauty

<u>Standalone Titles</u>
A Touch of Summer
Black Velvet
His Secret Obsession
Dirty Boy
Naughty Little Elf
Tempted by December
Devil's Deceit
A Bride for the Beast (writing with Fern Fraser)
A Hero for Her
Pretty Little Mess
Dear Mr. Dad Bod

<u>Easy on Me</u>
Easy Ride
Easy Surrender

<u>One Night with You</u>
Falling Hard
Model Behavior
Learning Curve
Angel Kisses

<u>Silver Spoon MC</u>
The Surgeon
The Heir
The Lawyer
The Prodigy
The Bodyguard
Silver Spoon MC Collection: Nichole's Crew

<u>Silver Spoon Falls</u>
Xavier's Kitten
Callum's Hope
Snow's Prince
Aurora's Knight

<u>Silver Spoon Falcons</u>
Leia's Playmaker
Aspen's Defense (coming soon)
Gabbi's Goalie (coming soon)

<u>writing with Loni Ree as Loni Nichole</u>
Dillon's Heart
Razor's Flame
Ryker's Reward
Zane's Rebel
Oral Arguments
Grizz's Passion
Garrett's Obsession

About Nichole Rose

Nichole Rose writes filthy romance for curvy readers. Her books feature headstrong, sassy women and the alpha males who consume them. From grumpy detectives to country boys with attitude to instalove and over-the-top declarations, nothing is off-limits.

Nichole is sure to have a steamy, sweet story just right for everyone. She fully believes the world is ugly enough without trying to fit falling in love into a one-size-fits-all box.

When not writing, Nichole enjoys fine wine, cute shoes, and everything supernatural. She is happily married to the love of her life and is a proud mama to the world's most ridiculous fur-babies. She and her husband live in Arkansas.

You can learn more about Nichole and her books at authornicholerose.com.

f
facebook.com/AuthorNicholeRose/

instagram.com/AuthorNicholeRose

twitter.com/AuthNicholeRose

BB
bookbub.com/authors/nichole-rose

tiktok.com/@authornicholerose